# POSSESSED BY A VAMPIRE

## IMMORTAL HEARTS OF SAN FRANCISCO BOOK 4

## SUSAN GRISCOM

www.susangriscom.com

Facebook

Edited by Michelle Leah Olson - Literally Addicted to Detail
Edited by Tami Lund
Proofed by: Trallee Mendonca

# NOTE TO READERS

Thank you so much for downloading Possessed by a Vampire. This is the fourth book in the Immortal Hearts of San Francisco Series and if you haven't read the first three books yet, you might want to go back and get those first. Though, this book can stand on its own, I believe you will want to get to know the other characters as well, as they all have a role in each of the books, though I've tried very hard not to give away any spoilers.

Possessed by a Vampire contains a lot of stuff that I'm sure some of my readers are not used to reading in my books. This book is very complicated because of the drug and human/vampire trafficking. I hope I got everything right.

Each book in this series is, and will be, written as a stand-alone and it shouldn't be necessary to read them in order, however, if you are as OCD as I am about reading series in order, then you should definitely do that.

Reading Order:

*Tempted by a Vampire*, Book 1, Cian & Magdalena
*Captivated by a Vampire*, Book 2, Chelle & Josh
*Rocked by a Vampire*, Book 3, Lane & Vanessa

*Possessed by a Vampire,* Book 4, Elvis & Lily
*Protected by a Vampire,* Book 5, Gage &Ace
*Bewitched by a Vampire,* Book 6, Lane & Vanessa again

The theme of The Immortal Hearts of San Francisco series came to me after soul searching for the perfect setting. I live close to San Francisco and some of my most memorable moments happened there. What better place to have rock and roll vampires than in the city where I left my heart?

I hope you enjoy reading about Elvis, aka Preston and Lily.

# DESCRIPTION

**They possess the power to make their dreams come true—but it won't be easy**.

Preston Knight—Elvis to his friends—loves being a vampire. The night he was turned was the first step to him becoming the kind of man he always hoped to be. Now, he's a rock star. What could be better? But the one thing that would make his world complete is just out of reach. The woman he yearns for has some serious secrets, and despite him knowing that she wants him just as much as he wants her, she won't let him in.

Lily Grey never asked to be a vampire. The choice was taken from her eons ago, and things never improved. Now, she finds herself peddling drugs on the streets of San Francisco and playing the part of doting wife to a possessive and sadistic vampire with delusions of grandeur. But family means everything to Lily, and she's willing to sacrifice everything for it . . . even her one chance at happiness with the sexy-as-sin vampire who sets her heart ablaze.

When one night of passion opens the door for a century of secrets to be revealed, Lily and Preston must fight for not only what they believe in but also what they love.

# CHAPTER 1

Elvis

"It's up to you, Elvis." Lincoln, the dealer, nodded in my direction and waited. I kept my gaze trained on the center of the table where chips sat in a small pile. I didn't need to look at my cards again. I knew what I had: an eight and a queen of hearts.

There were six vampires at the table, counting both Gage and me. Gage had folded right after the deal, and so had one of the other players. I was the last to bet, and sometimes I liked to spice things up a bit, so I matched the bet and sat back.

Heavy smoke hung in the air like delicate streams of fog, swirling in circled patterns under the light hanging from a long cord above the table. Four other lamps hung on fixtures attached to the otherwise stark, tawny brown walls. Even with all the bulbs, the room seemed dark.

Maybe it was the darkness of the souls in the room. I wasn't sure.

A droning sound buzzed from outside. It was a little annoying, but I managed to drown it out as I nonchalantly watched the faces around the table as the dealer placed the three cards of the flop face-up, revealing a nine of hearts. He slowly separated them, sliding the top card off the nine to reveal a jack of hearts.

Holy fuck!

It was raining hearts for some reason, and I held two of them already. I held my breath, waiting to see the third card in the flop. The dealer slid the jack over. Crap, an eight of diamonds.

Not exactly what I was looking for, but a pair of eights with a queen high wasn't completely a loss so I decided to hang in there and see if one more heart would show. There were still two cards to go, and a flush was possible.

I kept my eyes straight, my thoughts blank—or I tried—like I usually did as each card was revealed, always attempting to keep my composure, never deviating from the norm, not wanting to give away my emotions. I was an expert at reading people. Especially in a poker game. A blink of an eye, a slight twitch, a swallow, the slightest move-ment, anything . . . different could give someone's hand away. I wanted to reach up and finger my shades that sat on top of my head. Just one little nudge and they'd be sitting comfortably on my face, shielding my eyes. But not only were dark glasses frowned upon in this high-stakes game of Texas Hold 'em, but any movement out of the ordinary might tip someone off about my cards.

This wasn't our normal gathering with my brothers at the mansion. This was a high roller, unsanctioned but heavily guarded poker game with some seriously high-powered city officials that I'd bet my right nut were a drug cartel of some sort or another. The two thugs in the monkey suits positioned on either side of the door to the entrance had stood like statues most of the night; the bulge of a holster protruding from under their jackets an obvious clue. At least they were on the outside of the room, but they still remained at the ready if their services were required.

Gage and I didn't normally seek out games with such high stakes, but he'd been bored lately, and when he ran into Lincoln—the game's host—at Club Royal a couple of weeks ago, Lincoln had invited Gage and me to join. Said they'd recently lost two of their regulars and needed a couple of fill-ins.

When Gage had approached me, I shrugged him off at first, not wanting any part of something that sounded so sketchy. But after he'd pestered me for the entire week, I finally gave in, needing a distraction from the long hours—sometimes days—apart from Lily, the sexy and sweet vampire I'd been trying to get to know better. Except, for the past few months, she was either playing hard to get, or just wasn't that interested in me. Though I had a difficult time believing the latter of those two options since she continued to meet me whenever she had the time or, in her words, "could get away." Away from what, I hadn't been able to find out. Yet.

Getting thoughts of Lily off my mind was nearly impossible. Her fair, silky-smooth skin; her mesmerizing dark coffee eyes that could hold my gaze for hours on end; the tips of her long, thick locks kissing the cleavage of her breasts where my lips longed to skim. I managed to clear my head just in time, as it was my turn to bet again. I slid my bet forward, raising the pot three thousand for appearance's sake. In truth, without another heart or a ten, I had squat. I didn't think the pair of eights would cut it. I had an excellent chance for a straight or a flush if either of the next two cards went my way. Since Gage had already folded, he sat still as a statue beside me, his hands together on the edge of the table. I knew he was busting a gut wondering what I held in my hand.

There were only four of us left in this hand, and I didn't want to go home with a loss. Not against these guys. Two of them sat puffing on brown cigarettes, looking rather tough. They *were* tough, the sort who would drain the blood from a homeless person and leave them to die in the gutter without so much as a "thank you, ma'am." Particularly, the one at the end with the light brown, wool Stetson on his head. The word *dangerous* exuded from his pores. He wore that hat pulled low on his brow, shading his eyes just enough to where it was legal but not enough to reveal much about him. A neatly trimmed goatee graced his chin and upper lip. A long ponytail made of cornrow braids hung down his back. He seemed on edge, or maybe it was just an act to throw me off.

Which he did when he raised another five thousand. That was steep. Not that I didn't have the money. These days, my bank account overflowed, but it wasn't that way in the beginning. I hadn't always been the man I was today, and money hadn't been abundant back then. The circumstances surrounding my rebirth as a vampire weren't something I would likely forget, though I'd never spoken about them, not even to Gage. The way I'd been turned hadn't exactly been conventional vampire behavior and had left an ache in my soul I didn't understand and an emptiness that I could never satisfy.

I peeked at my cards and considered the raise. Either the guy had something powerful, or he was bluffing his ass off and had nothing. Since I had the queen of hearts, I knew he couldn't have a royal flush. But that didn't rule out a straight or four of a kind. The bald-headed guy next to him folded, as did the next two. Now it was up to me, and six thousand was just about all I had left in chips, so I shoved the entire stack I had into the middle of the table.

"I'm all in," I said with feigned confidence.

After the bet had been matched, the dealer flipped the fourth card.

A fucking nine of spades.

Shit.

I watched out of the corner of my eye as cowboy hat's mouth curved up on one side, the tip of his fang biting into his lower lip. Could mean he was nervous. Or cocky. Either way, my hand was dead unless a ten or another heart showed up.

My heart skipped a beat when the fifth card was flipped over. There it was, sparkling as if someone had lit it on fire. I managed to keep my composure as I chilled, though I could have sworn I heard fireworks go off outside.

The beautiful ten of hearts.

Stetson vamp chuckled and said, "Too bad. You played a nice hand." Then he laid down his cards. A pair of nines, giving him four of a fucking kind, which would beat most hands. When he started to grab at the pile of chips, I cleared my throat.

"Hold on there, space cowboy," I heard myself say, not sure if the cockiness in my voice would help or hinder, but that pile of chips in the center of the table belonged to me, and there was no fucking way I was letting this douche have them. I had a fucking straight flush, queen high. *Beat that you fucking cocksucker*. I wanted to gloat but managed to keep my cool and simply turned the two cards in my hand over and placed them face up on the table.

His face paled, if that were possible. His dark-stubbled jaw flexed. His eyes narrowed to slits. His left ear twitched, and he placed both his palms on the table as he stood, glaring at me. Everyone sitting around the table stiffened. The chips lay in a heap in the middle. He kept his large, ebony eyes on mine, gaze never faltering. I allowed myself to stare right back, not moving a centimeter. I was good at stare-out games. I'd had a cat, many in fact, and we constantly used to play this game. Stetson hat was no different in my mind. Though I was positive he thought differently. This guy was too fucking arrogant for my taste. I'd wondered from the moment I sat down if he was going to be trouble.

"Jace, you ready?" he barked.

The guy at the end of the table—Jace, I assumed—nodded. "Yep, I'm all tapped out. Ladies."

Stetson hat shrugged into a light brown wool coat, generously embellished with dark brown fur at the lapel, all the while keeping his gaze glued to me. "Be sure to join us again. I look forward to the opportunity to win that back." His eyes briefly averted to the large pile of chips in the middle of the table before returning to mine, and then he touched the rim of his hat and nodded like he was fucking Clint Eastwood. "Gentlemen." He kept his lips tight as he turned and walked out. Stopping by another vampire on his way, he looked down at him, made some sort of gesture with his hand, and left the room. Jace, and two other large vampires went with him.

Gage cleared his throat. "Fuck, man. That was intense." The three dudes left at the table all sighed heavily.

The vampire that Stetson hat had gestured to stood up. "Roach would like you to join him at his employer's mansion." Roach? What

5

the fuck kind of person named their kid Roach? I almost laughed. The poor guy. No wonder he was so intense. "It is open to you any Friday evening. That is the night they entertain small groups. Midnight. Here's the address." He slipped me a card. I glanced down at the etching on the flat piece of metal.

It read:

SWEET'S DELICACIES
*Whatever your pleasure, we've got it.*
*Sweet Towers, Sky Deck.*


WHEN THE VAMPIRE LEFT, Gage grabbed the card from me. "Shit. Looks like he wants a rematch."

"Well, he isn't getting one," I retorted and threw the fancy card down on the table. This was over right now. I didn't want any part of whatever the fuck that guy was dealing.

"I wouldn't be so quick to pass on that invite if I were you, Elvis," Lincoln, the vampire who'd hosted the night's game, said. "That vampire works for Sweet, one of this city's most dominant and influential business owners. He has the support of the local labor board, as well as several other highfalutin bigwigs in the city. It's quite the honor to be invited, even if it was by his right-hand man. Sweet doesn't give out invitations to his private parties very often. And his parties don't have anything to do with card games, if you get my drift. Roach must have liked you." He winked.

I raised my eyebrows at Lincoln in question.

"You know. Sex, drugs. Those kinds of parties. Group or single, whatever you desire. Or so I've heard."

Whatever kind of parties, I wasn't into group sex or drugs. I had a woman, or at least a woman I wanted, as the vision of Lily's striking brown eyes set against her smooth, deep black hair floated through my mind I got to my feet and shrugged into my jacket. "Come on, Gage, let's split."

As Gage and I strolled down the sidewalk through the Tenderloin, we noticed a couple of ladies of the night hanging out on the adjacent corner.

"That was a grueling hand. Made me a tad thirsty, what about you?" Gage asked.

I shrugged. "Sure, I guess."

I was a bit dry since I hadn't taken in any fresh blood for a day or so, but I wasn't sure I wanted to take the time to quench my thirst right at that moment as visions of Lily's lovely face floated into my head. It was difficult to shake them away because I was excited to get to the bar where we usually met, hoping she would be waiting there for me.

But Gage's suggestion sparked a need I hadn't considered, and I gave in. As we flashed across the street directly in front of the two women Gage quickly compelled both of them to not be alarmed by our sudden appearances. Then he sank his fangs into the neck of the one closest to him. The other stood still, staring blankly at me. My own fangs dropped at the thought of drinking her blood. As I sank my canines into her vein, I had to remind myself that I needed the energy this would provide me in order to fully enjoy my time with Lily without the annoying pang of hunger distracting me.

# CHAPTER 2

Lily

"Here's fifty." Malik held out a purple velvet bag, secured at the top by a satin pull rope.

"Fifty? I can't take fifty. Please, Malik, I can barely handle thirty." I stood from the chair I'd been sitting in waiting for Malik to bring me the newest batch.

"Boss says he wants it all gone before the next shipment comes in, which is tomorrow. You get fifty." His long, mocha-colored fingers fisted around the top of the bag, shoving it against my chest. "Take it. Don't make me have to report negatively back to him about you." His compassionate black orbs softened as he spoke in a deep, rich baritone. "I don't want to do that any more than you want me to. So take it and get to work." His smooth, dark face glistened under the lights of the chandelier hanging from the ceiling of the entrance I waited in. Or maybe it was sweat. Malik was a gentleman, but also someone highly devoted to Dorian. Or maybe he was simply scared of the powerful vampire as much as I was. It didn't matter. Both Malik and I had our roles to play. His was to do Dorian's grunt work; mine was to pretend to love him. Malik had the sleeves of his light blue sweater shoved up to his elbows, exposing his muscular, inked forearms. The skin at his wrists was encircled by scars from years of wearing heavy iron shackles as a slave on an English merchant ship transporting blacks from Africa during the seventeen hundreds. Malik's white teeth gleamed as he gave me a soft, encouraging smile. "You can do this." Then, without skipping a beat, he vanished from my sight, leaving me alone with my plight of figuring out how to dispense this much heroin in such a small amount of time.

I glanced at the antique, wooden grandfather clock standing against the far wall as it struck eleven times. It loomed there like a giant time bomb warning me that I didn't have much time to find buyers for all these drugs. I sucked in my bottom lip as I took in a deep breath and reluctantly held the bag. I had three hours to sell almost twice as much heroin as normal, and I had no clue where I would be able to find that many junkies, especially in my usual territory. I'd never taken drugs, and I hated that I was forced to sell them, but I should probably be grateful that Dorian hadn't yet used me as one of the other commodities he traded. *Traded* was a mild word. Sold. As in slavery.

I could escape easily enough. Hide away some place far away from Dorian and his minions, but it wasn't just me I had to think of.

I glanced at the bag in my hand and thought of Julian.

I had to do this for Julian.

I was going to need to cover more ground tonight, so I took off toward the wharf and materialized behind one of the older warehouses along the waterfront, staying far away from the expensive and elegant restaurants. Most of the people at the wharf were tourists, but at this time of night, I was sure I'd be able to locate some needy vagrants looking for the perfect high.

"You're pretty brave to be out here alone, missy." I turned to see a man leaning against the gray brick wall of the building, dressed in black, his dark hood shielding most of his head. I frowned, immediately tuned in to his body language, and it wasn't drugs he was looking for. You could almost see the thoughts of sex circling out of control in his head, desire glinting from his eyes. Lust practically dripped from his lips. "What's a pretty girl like you doing out here this late?" he said, pushing himself off the wall with the heel of the boot he'd had pressed against it. He took a few steps towards me, and my stomach groaned.

I was hungry, not having had time for any nourishment before Malik gave me the large satchel of drugs to distribute. In fact, it had been a week since I'd last fed from a human. Fresh blood was always preferred, but when you were locked in a room and unable to leave, one must take whatever provisions were allotted.

The man stank of booze as he stood a few inches from me, his smile arrogant as he held up a large knife and waited for my reaction.

Silly human rapist.

Before he even knew what had happened, the knife was on the ground, and I had him backed up against the wall he'd been leaning on so casually moments before. I sank my fangs deep into his throat, filling myself with much-needed sustenance. His arms dangled at his sides, twitching as I drank. I considered draining the creep, but I'd never actually killed anyone before and I wasn't about to start tonight. I stopped sucking and licked his wounds closed.

I stared into his dark, bloodshot eyes and activated my compulsion ability. "I could kill you. I *should* kill you. But instead, I have something else in mind. You will never, ever rape another woman. You will become violently ill whenever the thought of sex enters your mind. If your dick gets hard, you will cry like a baby and throw up all over yourself. You will be kind to every female you encounter, and you will volunteer all of your time gathering donations to help victims of rape and other domestic violence. Do you understand?"

"Yes." His whimper was barely audible.

"Good." I grabbed at his dirty crotch and stroked against the rough, denim material to witness my cunning idea in action. A whimpering sound escaped from his throat, and tears poured from his eyes. I quickly jumped aside as vomit oozed from his mouth and down the front of his shirt. "Good," I repeated. "That is excellent."

I disappeared, removing myself from that disgusting encounter, and materialized down at the beach where a few bonfires were lit. As I approached a small group of what appeared to be homeless people— two shopping carts filled with black plastic bags and other miscellaneous items being my clue—gathered around one of the fires. I recognized one of the males. He was a regular customer of mine. I sighed with relief. If anyone were able to help me push this large amount of heroin, it would be Lenny.

JUST AS I'D HOPED, Lenny had managed to help me sell all but two bags down on the beach. Why I hadn't ever thought to go down there before was mind-boggling. From now on, the beach would be my salvation as well as my good fortune.

It was nearing two in the morning as I headed back up toward the Tenderloin district and The I.V., the bar where I hoped Preston would be waiting for me. Seeing Press was a dangerous endeavor, knowing Dorian would have my head as well as Julian's if he ever found out.

I still had a couple of bags left to sell, and as I rounded the corner to the bar, I happened upon a couple of addicts whose names escaped me. I'd sold to them before, though, and it was my good luck that they looked like they could use a fix. One wore a brown windbreaker and khaki pants that looked as if he'd pulled them out of a dumpster. His dirty, stringy hair hung down over his eyes. Totally disgusting. The other man, though equally dirty, was mostly bald and had on jeans ripped at the knees, and a well-worn, black leather jacket with enough cracks in it to make it look like elephant skin.

"Hey, girlie, we've been waiting for you," the black leather jacket guy said.

My nose automatically wrinkled from the stench of the men as I stood a few inches in front of them. I doubted either of them had taken a shower for at least a week. I almost felt sorry for them and considered—very briefly—turning them into vamps just to remove them from their current miserable existence. But I'd never done that. Besides, I had a date waiting for me. Hopefully.

"What's a girl like you doing peddling this shit anyway? Don't you worry about getting raped?" Baldy asked.

I considered his question. I could tell him that I was a vampire—one whose sole purpose out here was to protect someone else—and thus the chances of being raped were minimal. But then they'd just laugh, thinking I was joking. So I simply smiled. "What do you care as long as I have stuff for you?"

He shrugged and showed me some gross, yellow teeth. "Don't care. Just being friendly, I guess."

"Don't be. Just give me the money, and I'll give you your shit."

They both reached into their pockets and pulled out small wads of cash, offering them to me. I took the bundles and counted. "This one is short seventy dollars," I said, holding up the one in my left hand.

"That's all I got," stringy hair guy claimed, shrugging his shoulders again and wiping his fingers across his nostrils, sniffling.

Again, my heart strings pulled for the guy a bit, but dammit, I needed *all* the cash when I returned tonight, or I'd have to deal with a punishment I wasn't sure I could endure.

I sighed and put the cash in my purse and handed them the bags. I'd have to find another way to get that extra seventy before I returned. Stringy hair guy looked at me with quizzical, tired, and too-old-for-his-young-age eyes.

I waved them away. "Go on. Get out of here before I change my mind."

"Thanks," he said, shoving the stash inside his jacket as they both hurried away.

I had no idea how I would make up the shortage, but I was relieved that I'd been successful at ridding myself of the entire amount of heroin.

Now that I'd managed to finally sell all the drugs, I ached to see Preston, and I hoped he'd still be at The I.V., the bar where we usually met. It was a dive frequented primarily by vampires, a run-down tavern in the less fortunate Tenderloin district of the city, and feeding was easier there because of the vagrants and hookers. I'd met Press by accident a few months ago as I'd sat at the bar. I'd gone in there after I managed to get rid of that night's shipment just to relax for a few minutes before heading back home. I'd been killing time, waiting for the night to pass, not wanting to go back to Dorian's just yet, and Preston had come in and sat down next to me. I instantly recognized him as one of the band members from the Lost Boys who played at Club Royal. When Preston had turned to me and questioned why I was in such a sleazy place like The I.V., I simply shrugged. But then he removed his shades, and I glanced into his mysterious dark eyes that instantly melted my heart. From that moment on, I wanted to know more about him, and desperately wished I didn't need to return to Dorian. But as the night progressed after introductions, and Preston and I talked, Dorian became the last thing on my mind. Press and I chatted and laughed together until it was almost daylight. We've been meeting there a few nights a week ever since.

When I finally did make it home, Dorian wasn't even there, which I was thankful for. Whenever Dorian was home, every night was a party. He was continually inviting people over to make deal after deal.

I flashed to the alley behind the bar where I usually entered through the back door. Right after I materialized, two large men came around the corner. They didn't look very friendly, and I didn't want to stick around to find out for sure, so I hurried inside.

My stomach jittered with excitement at the sight of him sitting at the counter alone, his finger slowly skimming the edge of the tumbler in front of him, and his black leather jacket unzipped and open to reveal a black silk shirt. His dark glasses were down over his eyes, and he hadn't seen me come in yet. He looked mysterious and sexy, and I wanted so badly to lay with him in private. To feel his hands on my body was just a dream, though, as I didn't want to involve him in any of my problems. Dorian was a dangerous man, and I couldn't afford to have Preston become one of his enemies. Preston and I had kissed a few times, but I'd been reluctant to let things go any further for fear of Dorian finding out. I needed to keep Press a secret. Of course, I knew if Dorian ever found out about my relationship with Preston, he'd kill not only me but also Julian—maybe Preston, too.

No, for now, Dorian needed to believe and trust that I belonged to him and only him. If I ever acted on my desires for Preston, I was certain that Dorian would know—he'd see right through me. There was no way I could hide my feelings for Preston if we were to take our friendship to the next level.

"You have beautiful eyes. Why do you always hide behind those dark shades?"

"Lily." Preston turned toward me and gave me a delicious smile. "You made it." He raised his glasses to reveal the most gorgeous, dark chocolate eyes I'd ever seen; eyes I found myself frequently lost in. Securing his black lenses on his head, he pulled the stool next to him closer. "Please, sit. I've been wondering if you would be here tonight. I'm glad you came."

I smiled. "How are you, Preston?"

"Better, now that you're here." He spoke softly, his mouth close to my ear. His breath was spiced like the whiskey he'd been drinking, and I wanted to turn my face and press my lips against his.

Did he feel the same way? Renewed, youthful, and lightheaded with desire? Being close to Preston made me want to run naked on the beach with him, holding hands as we fell blissfully to the sand in each other's arms and made passionate love. Butterflies took flight in my stomach whenever he was near, but I kept that all to myself for fear of leading him on to something I couldn't allow or chance.

The bartender placed a glass of red wine in front of me without asking what I wanted. It was my usual. I didn't think I'd ever ordered anything other than wine, and this old vine zin they had here lately was excellent.

"I was hoping you'd come by tonight. I wanted to let you know I'm taking the lead tomorrow night at the club. I thought you might like to come and listen. I can reserve a table for you."

I smiled. I'd heard Preston play before and he was fantastic. He'd done a couple of Elvis Presley numbers from the late sixties. His bandmates even called him Elvis. Though he had introduced himself to me as Preston. He told me that Elvis was a nickname they'd given him because he wore those dark glasses all the time and, of course, his name being Preston, they'd begun calling him Elvis Presley. "I will, on one condition," I said, though I hadn't a clue as to how I would get out. But I'd done it before; I would try again.

"What's that?"

"I'd like to see you perform something as Preston. You introduced yourself to me as Preston, and it's that guy I want to see on stage."

He grinned. "That, I can absolutely do. No problem." To my surprise, he stood and grabbed my hand. "Come with me a minute."

I stood and followed him through a door leading to a hallway where the restrooms were and then to another heavy, metal door. Press shoved the door open and gestured for me to go outside. As I stepped into the cool night air, someone large stepped out of the shadows, grabbed me by my arms, and tugged me against them.

I gasped as the unexpected assailant held me with my back against him and his hand around my throat in a tight grasp. I tugged at his arm, but by the strength of his hold, I instantly recognized that he was a vampire. I'd never been attacked in an alleyway by a vampire before and it took me completely by surprise.

"Nice of you to come out here and join me, missy," he hissed against my ear. His breath smelled like dead rats, and I wondered if he'd recently fed on one.

As Preston stepped through the door, he stopped in his tracks at the sight of me being held by that creep. His eyes narrowed, his mouth tightened, and he stood ready to fight. I grasped my hands around the vampire's arm again and tugged with all my strength, finally freeing myself from his chokehold. Preston immediately pulled me away from the idiot vampire and tucked me behind him, shielding me with his body.

"Hey, I saw her first," the vampire said. As I peeked over Press's shoulder at the guy, it clicked. He was one of the two men who'd approached the bar right after I materialized back here earlier. I'd been right about them being unfriendly, though *unfriendly* was being kind. This one was creepy looking with gaunt, hollow cheeks, rather cadaverous in appearance. He flashed blood-stained teeth as he grinned at me. He *did* look as if he fed on rats regularly.

"She's not available," Preston growled through gritted teeth.

I could have taken care of the idiot myself, but I enjoyed watching Preston zip into protective mode as his foot met my attacker's jaw, sending him flying backwards against the wall. Everything seemed under control until the second vampire who had been with him earlier came out of the shadows. He was uglier and meaner looking than the first one, with two huge black eyes that bugged out like a giant fly's, and a mouth the size of . . . well, it was freaking huge. I would have loved to have something to shove into that massive maw to shut his ugly trap.

"Carl, get the fuck up," uglier vampire yelled at his friend. "I told you to wait for me, stupid." Then he turned toward us. "Come on." He wiggled his fingers at Preston, urging him to come at him. "Let's see how you do against two of us."

He lunged at Preston with clenched fists flying, but Press was fast and ducked low. From his crouched stance, he swung his leg up. His booted foot caught the ugly vampire right in his too-big mouth, making him stagger backwards, but he quickly regained his balance.

As Preston fought the ugly vampire, hollow cheeks got to his feet and came at me. I twisted and kicked him in the middle of his chest. He hardly noticed and came back for more. I tried for another kick, but his hand caught my leg and I toppled backwards, almost falling to the ground. I took advantage of my momentum and back-kicked him hard in the jaw. He went flying right into ugly vampire's swinging fist meant for Preston, slamming him hard against the wall. I immediately kicked him in the head one more time as he crumbled to the ground, completely out cold.

I turned to see Preston pummel punch after punch into ugly vamp's face, and without skipping a beat, Press picked him up with hardly any effort and tossed him clear across the alley. The ugly vampire slammed against the brick wall then slid to the pavement. Press wasn't out of the ordinary large, but his vampire strength outshined most others I've witnessed. He wasn't only a great musician; apparently, he was also a badass fighter, and I may have just fallen a bit deeper for him—if that were even possible.

"Let's go back inside. It's a little too crowded out here," he said and wrapped his arm around my waist as we walked back into the hallway of the bar. He tugged me to a stop midway and gently shoved me against the wall, positioning himself in front of me, his hands pressed against the brick beside my head. His gaze caught mine in a sensual stare, his large body shielding me . . . from everything except him. When he skimmed his finger down my cheek and along my jawbone, I closed my eyes and pressed my face into his hand.

"Lily."

I melted at the sound of my name uttered in his rich, throaty voice. I opened my eyes to see his beautiful heat-filled gaze captivating me and I felt as if I were under his spell. I was. The magic of his desire made me want to forget all about Dorian and the danger he posed.

"I'm sorry about those jerks out back. I didn't know they were out there or I would never have let you go out first."

I shook my head. "You have nothing to be sorry for. You had no idea they were there. Besides, lucky for me, you were with me."

"I'll always protect you."

Preston's lips pressed against mine, and within a few seconds, everything around us dissolved. I found myself opening to him, pulling him closer to me. Wanting more. Unable to deny the pleasure of his taste, I melted as his tongue slipped between my parted lips, and his fingers played against the nape of my neck. His digits tangled in my curls, while his other hand splayed against my lower back. Lost in his embrace, his body so firm against mine, I placed my hand over his chest, skimming my fingers over the taut muscles just inside his black shirt. I wanted to touch him, to experience everything that he was. I'd never been kissed the way Preston kissed me. There was so much passion and need behind every movement. My breathing became heavy. I wanted him more than I wanted to breathe. But as much as I desired him, the power of what would happen if I allowed him to take me the way I wanted, no . . . *needed* to be taken became too overwhelming. I could do major damage to human creeps like the one in the alley earlier tonight, or vampires like Hallow Cheeks, but I was nothing but putty in this sexy man's arms.

When he stopped kissing my mouth, his lips trailed down my neck.

"Please, Preston," I huffed out between breaths. "We can't."

"Lily, we've been meeting now for three months. I don't understand you. Every time we kiss, you stop us before we can even get started. You allow yourself to feel. Your desire for me is evident, yet you won't allow yourself to enjoy what I know you want. Let me take you away from whatever it is you fear."

"I can't."

"Tell me why."

I shook my head as uncontrollable tears dripped down my cheeks. "I can't."

"Lily, whatever it is that's making you cry, keeping you from being with me, I will crush it. Trust me. There's nothing in this world too big, too difficult. Let me help you. Please."

I wanted to trust him. I wanted him to take me away from all the pain and suffering, but I couldn't bring myself to trust the fact that Dorian wouldn't harm him the way I knew he could.

"I do trust you, but I can't be with you this way. Please just accept that for now. *Trust me*," I countered. "I want to be with you, I do. Someday, we will be together. I promise. But for now, please."

"I worry about you. I can't stop thinking about you. Let me take you somewhere right now."

"I don't have much time."

"It won't take long. You can leave whenever you like. Just let me show you something."

"Where to?"

"Trust me."

He picked me up and cradled me in his arms as he flashed us to a large, flat, metal slab. As I quickly glanced around, I realized that we were in the middle of the ocean, high above the water on some sort of metal platform. Waves rolled and licked the rocks below as I looked back at the coastline, which from my view, seemed to be miles away.

"Where are we?"

"We're on the top of the Mile Rocks Lighthouse. It literally sits in the middle of the ocean on a bed of concrete and rock. Though it's not a lighthouse anymore. They removed the lamp and lenses that were on top of here. Now, it's used for helicopter landings."

"Who in the hell would want to land a helicopter on top of this, in the middle of the ocean? Where would they go?"

He laughed.

"I have no idea. But I come here all the time, and I've never seen one land. Maybe they do that more in daylight."

The wind was strong and cold, and I began to shiver. "Why do you come here?" I asked as I wrapped my arms around myself.

He pulled me close, enveloping me in his embrace. "I'm sorry, I should have thought about how cold it was before I brought you here." He released me and shrugged out of his jacket to drape it around my body before wrapping his arms back around me. "It's peaceful here with no noise from the city. I usually sit on the edge and let my legs dangle over the side. I come here mostly just to think, when I have important things to ponder. I've been coming here a lot lately."

He lifted my chin up with his finger as his mouth captured mine again. I let his kiss take hold of me, and imprinted the softness of his lips on my memory. I never wanted to forget how amazing they felt. My breath hitched as his hand splayed across my stomach. As his fingers skimmed up to take my breast in his palm, I tensed. As much as I wanted to let this go further, as much as I wanted him to take me right here on this . . . metal contraption in the middle of the Pacific Ocean, fear enveloped me. I needed him to stop. "Please, Preston." I slowly stepped out of his embrace. "I need to go. I'm so sorry."

19

# CHAPTER 3

Elvis, aka Preston

*M*ultiple rays of fluorescent light filtered through the heavy smoke inside Club Royal—one of the few places left in San Francisco where smoking was still allowed. What the fuck did we care? It wasn't like we'd die of lung cancer. Hell, three quarters of the patrons were vampires who didn't give a rat's ass about health issues. Most of them were here to hook up for blood and sex. And a lot of them smoked. Personally, I'd never liked the taste of tobacco, but I didn't mind the smoke.

Sweat dripped down my back as I strutted across the stage, my guitar secure in my hands. My fingers strummed the first chords, and *Crazy* resounded from my lips as if I were Steven Tyler himself. Everyone had expected *Jail House Rock*, but I wasn't in the mood for Elvis. They'd all been prepared for it, but the quick song change had been quickly recognized by Lane, Cian, and Gage, and they were all able to keep up. I knew they would.

I once had the pleasure of jammin' with both of those legendary artists—Tyler and Presley. Back in the days of Elvis, it was cool to have long side burns and short-cropped hair that flopped over my forehead whenever I bopped my head to the beat. All the women adored me back then. Don't get me wrong, they still loved me, and I never had any problem in that area. Ever. I guess I did look a bit like the king of rock and roll whenever I donned the dark glasses and tugged up the collar of my black shirt with the sleeves rolled up the way the real Elvis used to do. And when I started gyrating my hips, every woman within viewing distance screamed as if they were having the orgasm of their lives.

These days, I still kept my hair short, but without the long side burns. People changed, and I was no exception. I still wore the dark shades, though. It was a necessity where I was concerned. Sunscorched eyes were no fun, so I was always prepared. I've gotten caught out in the sunlight a few times—not long enough to do any damage—so I always liked to be prepared. But the shades were just the beginning. My leather jacket had recently been magically altered to protect me from the sun's brutal rays, as well, thanks to a certain powerful witch I knew. Except that didn't do much for my head or the lower portion of my body. It wasn't the best protection, but it was good enough to keep my energy from being drained until I could get back inside.

Sunlight is a vampire's kryptonite, rendering us helpless. If we stayed out in it too long, it could kill us. It wouldn't disintegrate us instantly like in the movies, but, if all your energy dissipated through your skin as if your pores were a sieve, you'd surely die. Though I didn't know of any vamp who'd actually died from sun exposure. I did, however, know that it hurt like a son of a bitch to get caught out in it. And I heard it did nasty things to your organs if major dehydration occurred.

I belted out the last chorus and had the thought that Steven Tyler would have been proud. I glanced at Cian, and he swiped his hand across his throat, giving me the signal that it was break time.

"Thank you!" I shouted into the microphone. "Thank you very

21

much," I added in true Elvis fashion. Everyone loved it. "We're the Lost Boys, and we'll be right back after a short break."

Moans and groans came from the crowd, and I glanced out into the audience, searching. A sigh of relief flowed through me as I saw those mesmerizing, beautiful cognac eyes, and almost black, long, wavy hair. Lily smiled up at me and waved as a tingle swept through my balls. I wanted to fuck her so badly. I'd waited to have her for the last few months, but she wouldn't have it, and I wasn't an asshole about it. Vampire women were usually so free with their bodies, but not Lily. I sort of liked that about her, even though my balls grew blue whenever I was around her.

She'd left me in such a hurry last night, I wasn't sure she'd be here tonight. I wanted to dispense with the no-mingling-with-patrons-during-intermission rule and go to her, but my brothers were important to me. I respected them, and they respected me. It was usually too distracting and too difficult to pry some of the women away from us. We didn't stray from our directives unless we were all in agreement. But Lily wasn't their concern or business, and I wasn't about to make it so. I just hoped she would still be sitting at that table when we returned to the stage.

"Hey, Elvis. What happened to *Jail House Rock*?" Lane asked me as we walked into the cool and spacious room behind the stage. The temperature in the room was always kept at around sixty degrees because when we got off the lighted stage, we needed to cool down.

Elvis was a nickname. One I'd never asked for, but the guys thought it would be a great stage name, and I went along with it. It never bothered me until recently. Mostly because Lily called me Press, or mostly Preston, my real name. I'd been born Preston Charles Knight. But I'd been Elvis for the past forty years or so when the four of us started performing together. Gage, Lane, and Cian were the other members of The Lost Boys. The name of the band had been Gage's idea after he watched the movie in the eighties. No one protested, so it stuck.

Lane grabbed the bottle of whiskey—his way of cooling off—and took a long pull on it as he plopped down in one of the four recliners in the room that flanked each side of the pool table in the middle of the space.

I shrugged and headed for the fridge and grabbed a bottle of ice-cold water. After chugging the entire thing, I crunched the bottle to a flat disk and tossed it in the recycling bin.

"I wasn't feeling the Elvis thing tonight."

"Hey, no big deal," Cian said, taking the bottle of whiskey from Lane.

"Hey!" Lane complained.

"You have to share, brother." Cian poured two fingers into a few of the glasses that sat on the table then passed one to me before lowering himself into the black leather recliner set off to the right side of the room.

"He was sick the day they learned to share in kindergarten," Gage joked.

Cian laughed and then added, "Sorry, Lane. I think Elvis needs the booze more than you do. So, El, what's going on? Anything you want to talk about?"

I leaned against the wall and swallowed some of the golden liquid.

"It's that sexy vamp he's been seeing. Lily," Gage supplied as he sat in one of the other chairs. "She won't let him in her pants."

I glared at Gage, wishing I could shoot fire daggers out of my eyes into his dead heart. I loved the guy, but sometimes he really knew how to get under my skin.

"You're just jealous because that chick, Jillian, took off for New York, leaving your sorry ass."

Gage flipped me off. "She had issues, man. Vanessa's cousin or not, it wasn't gonna work. She was in love with the idea of being in love. She wanted me to meet her fucking parents. Do I look like the kind of guy someone takes home to meet Mom and Dad?" he asked, shooting us all a wide-fanged grin. "I ended up putting her on a plane back to New York, but not before wiping her mind of me and everything that happened out here."

"Good thing." Cian nodded. "Someone like that could be detrimental to our well-being."

"Why waste your time with a girl who's holding out, Elvis? There's plenty of other hot and willing pussy out there tonight, and they're all waiting and wishing you'd strut your stuff all *over* theirs." Lane chuckled at his own self-proclaimed clever wit. His hair hung loosely over his shoulders to the middle of his back. A few of the short front straggler strands stuck to his forehead, drenched with sweat. He lifted one of his black leather-clad legs and propped his large booted foot on the chair beside him. Lane was the epitome of rock and roll with his black silk shirt open to his navel, exposing his pale, muscled chest. We all had our roles to play.

Cian on the other hand, was more subdued in appearance. He kept his hair cropped short and his jeans tight but clean. For twins, they were like night and day.

I let out a short laugh and took another drink from the half-empty tumbler I held. Lane was right. But, unfortunately, none of the women attached to those pussies had gorgeous eyes the color of cognac, a soft, tantalizing voice, or the silky-smooth skin that Lily had. The woman did something to me. I hadn't felt this way about a female in over . . . well, ever.

"He's got it bad for the flower chick," Gage said and ran his large hand through his long, blondish hair. Sweat beaded on Gage's forehead, and he took a paper towel from the table and wiped it over his face. "Fuck, Cian. What's wrong with the air conditioner? It's like a fucking furnace on stage tonight." Gage was a big guy. Bigger than the rest of us. Stronger, too. He'd recently taken to wearing black leather pants like Lane. I was surprised they made them that large. His hair was long too, though not as long as Lane's. I was a comfort freak. I liked my leather, but only as my jacket. My comfort and freedom of movement were priorities, so my jeans were soft, well worn, and dark.

"I know. I'll have Ari look into it," Cian supplied and snatched his phone from his pocket before he tapped a button and stepped away—to talk to Ari, I assumed.

Gage and I had become close back in the early sixties. July fourth, seventeen sixty-three to be exact. I'd been a fairly new vampire back then, and Gage, well, he was older than dirt and helped me get through some lonely times. He hadn't sired me. Though I wished he had. I'd been turned by a sex-starved vampire who thought it would be great to have a companion, but then left me without a friend in the world. I didn't know any other vampires, and becoming friends with humans was out of the question since all I'd wanted to do back then was suck on their veins.

Gage had spotted me one night, sitting alone in a dark, dismal little tavern, my shirt and face still bloody from a recent feeding. I'd been down and out, lonely too, and had never bothered to clean up after I fed. When he'd asked if he could join me, I simply shrugged.

He'd sat down across from me and told me it wasn't a good idea to walk around with my dinner still on my face and then inquired if I had a place to stay. I did, but I didn't want to go back there, so he offered me his place to clean up. We'd been together ever since. Gage and I were as close as any two brothers could be, maybe even as close as Cian and Lane, and that was pretty damn close considering they're twins.

"So, this Lily, does she live in the city?" Lane asked, bringing me out of my reverie.

I shook my head and headed toward the door without answering. Truth was, I had no idea where Lily lived, but I was anxious to see if she was still out in the audience. When I walked on stage and glanced at the table where she'd been sitting, the chair was empty.

# CHAPTER 4

Lily

$\mathcal{I}$'d left Preston at the lighthouse last night fearing we'd go too far if I stayed. I enjoyed his affection too much. Though, as I sat here tonight, watching him on stage, I wished I'd stayed with him. All the females in the club were crazy about him. He was the sexiest and nicest man-turned-vampire I had ever encountered. Something about him had me completely awed. He was kind, sweet, and also a badass when it came to protecting what was his. Each time we met, it just kept getting harder and harder to deny the need to be touched by him.

I slipped out of the club while the band was on break. I hated that I hadn't been able to get a message to Preston to tell him I needed to leave, but then I'd have to explain why. I couldn't tell Preston about Dorian, the vampire I lived with—whom I was supposed to be in love with, or rather pretend.

But Dorian had some special social engagement tonight that I needed to attend with him, and so I needed to leave.

I'd managed to sneak away from my room—or prison cell as I liked to think of it—by telling Malik that I still needed to sell a few of the bags I'd been saddled with last night. Malik said he would cover for me, knowing how much trouble I'd be in if I didn't get the full amount for the shipment.

When I left the bar and materialized back at Dorian's complex, no one was the wiser. I had returned just in time, too, shucking my dark purple, hooded coat a mere moment before I heard Dorian approaching my room.

I quickly messed up the covers on the bed as I heard him enter and yawned when he walked in as though I'd been resting. Pretending and hiding my emotions was difficult but necessary. If I let my guard down, he'd know immediately that I had been gone. I knew I'd never be able to hide my feelings from him if Preston and I ever took our relationship to the next level. Dorian was a monster that dealt in horrific matters. Someone I never wanted Preston to come in contact with. If Dorian ever found out where I snuck off to, I'd risk Preston's life, as well as the other members of the band—and Julian. That was the last thing I wanted to do.

I grabbed my coat, shrugging my arms back into it as I stepped toward Dorian when he came into my room, then placed my hand on his Kiton suit-clad chest as I gently shoved him back out the door. Luckily, I'd had the good sense to wear a cocktail dress to the club tonight, so I didn't need to change for Dorian's engagement.

"I've been waiting for you, Dorian," I said and then walked straight down the hall to the limo outside. I held my breath the entire way, not releasing it until he joined me inside the car and smiled at me, seemingly delighted at my feigned excitement at going to yet another chamber of commerce gala with too much alcohol and too many handsy men.

Two blocks into our ride, Dorian asked Jace to stop the car at a mini-mart.

"I want to get some smokes," he said as he left the car. I hated when he smoked. It was a good thing that the nicotine didn't bother vampires, or Dorian would have died from lung cancer years ago.

I needed to pull myself together. That had been too close. I'd almost been caught returning from the club and I needed a few minutes to collect myself. Preston had been magnificent. I loved that he'd taken my suggestion to heart and didn't perform an Elvis song first tonight. I knew he probably would in the second half of the show because that was his act. Everyone expected it. Everyone wanted it. I loved watching him perform, even when he was performing Elvis. But there was a part of me that wanted to see the real man inside. Elvis was an act, someone his friends told him he should be, and, unfortunately, I think the real Preston Knight became lost somewhere along the way. I was glad that I had gotten to see the real man behind the dark shades before I had to leave.

I needed a few minutes alone without Jace, so I decided to take advantage of the situation and pulled out a tube of lip gloss from the pocket of my coat before I stepped out of the car behind Dorian. He stopped, immediately catching my wrist with his hand. His grip was too tight and I winced from the pain, but he didn't let up.

"Where are you going?"

"Just to the restroom. I forgot to put some lip gloss on." I held up the tube as I straightened. "Don't be long. I don't want to be late."

"It'll just take a second, I promise." He released me and I hurried to the bathroom before he could argue with me. We were in a public place, and I knew he wouldn't use force on me when there was the possibility of witnesses. I stood at the small sink, dabbing a damp paper towel on my face and neck. The close call of almost getting caught had made my skin hot and clammy. I gave my cheeks one last pat with the towel, took a deep breath, exhaling slowly to calm my nerves, and headed back to the limo and luck was on my side as Dorian hadn't returned yet. The last thing I needed was him getting angry with me because I took too long in the restroom.

When Dorian re-entered the car, he sank back against the luxurious black leather of the limo's back seat and put his arm around me, pulling me against him. He had his long, black hair pulled away from his handsome face in a tight, neat ponytail that gave him the distinguished and prominent businessman image I was sure he was going for. It accentuated his chiseled jaw and was a change from his usual carefree style with his dark curls flowing down over his ears to his neck. He smelled of lavender and licorice—a nauseating combination —that made me gag on more than one occasion. Sitting in the back of the car was at least quiet and peaceful; a break from the constant party that seemed to follow Dorian around like a lost puppy. I'd actually been looking forward to the gala tonight. Going out to a party meant there wouldn't be a crazy orgy in the middle of the living room for once. After all, if Dorian wasn't there, there was no party.

"Babe, what's wrong?" I hated when he called me cute little nicknames. I wasn't his *babe*, nor would I ever be. I was simply a stand-in, a ruse to hide what he really was. "Why were you in such a hurry to leave tonight when I entered your room?" Dorian asked as he opened the mini fridge in the limo and pulled out two bags of blood. I shrugged, not wanting to fabricate another lie. He handed one of the bags to me, and I took it. Then he passed me a small straw that I poked through the tiny hole at the top of the bag. I didn't want to answer him so I just began sipping down the blood. "I'm sorry I was so late." He gently skimmed his finger down my cheek in a very un-Dorian-like manner, and I wanted to vomit at his touch, his false actions of affection made me sick. "Were you waiting long for me?"

I shook my head. "Not very long."

This was his way of consoling me so I'd perform admirably for him tonight; pretending to be the adoring wife Dorian thought he needed to prove he was a loving family man to all his business partners and supporters. He'd prance around with me on his arm, feigning his love. Maybe he was in love with me in some twisted fashion, but I was more of a possession. His love was hard and demented, and his vampiric life's ambitions were twisted. With Dorian, it was all about the money and his investments—right or wrong. He didn't care whom he stepped on along the way, and he didn't look back. Though most times I felt like a prisoner, he did take care of me—in his own demented way. I had a roof over my head, and blood to sustain me most days. This was my life, my destiny. I'd accepted it long ago. Though, lately, after spending time with

Preston, I was reminded once again how Dorian's ways were not normal.

The thought of Preston made me yearn for my freedom, and I rested my head on the back of the seat and closed my eyes, wishing things were different. Preston and I weren't a couple, though our desires for each other were strong. I had to fight mine constantly.

"Hey, you look sad. Did something happen tonight?" Dorian asked sweetly, breaking me out of my reverie. He came off so nice, a part of me wanted to tell him about Preston, except I knew his sugar was coated with venom.

"No. I'm fine. I just wish you'd gotten home a bit earlier," I lied.

He chuckled. "Anxious for a night out on the town?"

I nodded and smiled. Better he think I was excited about being out with him. My life was safer if he thought I enjoyed these events, giving the public a false sense of what type of man he actually was. I didn't like being out with Dorian, but I had no other options. I had to keep pretending, or I'd lose the one person who mattered more to me than my own life. I was in this for one reason: to free Julian. Dorian kept me for two things: public appearances, and because he knew he could get me to do practically anything as long as he held my brother captive.

One of the perks of being a vampire was the ability to shut down my mind and emotions. I could do this for Julian, even if I had to be a slave to the most powerful drug and human/vampire trafficking lord in San Francisco.

# CHAPTER 5

*L*ily was gone. Dammit. Gage followed my gaze as I stared at the empty seat in the audience. As I strapped on my guitar, he clapped me on the back. "Better luck next time, bro." Then he headed to the drums and sat on the stool. Picking up the sticks, he tapped them three times on the side of the bass drum, indicating the start of a song. I struck the first chord of *Jail House Rock* and went through the motions. When the song ended, I stepped back away from the microphone and let Lane take over. I was done.

Why did Lily keep putting me off? What kept her from being with me? There had to be something else going on in her life. But what? Shit, was she seeing someone else? But why would she keep meeting me, kissing me, acting as though she wanted to be with me, yet holding out? Maybe their relationship was on the rocks and she was scared to leave or afraid to take that final step to freedom. Maybe she just got out of a bad relationship and now she was afraid to try again. Fuck. Lily had to be involved with someone else. I only wished she'd be truthful with me. But my guess was that it was someone not to be tested or trusted. That was the vibe I got. I knew we weren't actually dating, even though I liked to think we were. We'd only kissed a couple of times. I'd hoped she'd come to her senses and leave whoever he was so she would be free to be with me, but I didn't want to over-step any boundaries and push her—even though I sensed that her relationship with whomever she was with wasn't exactly a bed of roses. There had never been a woman whose mere presence excited me as Lily's did. I'd almost forgotten how to be civil to a proper woman, since most of the women Gage and I brought home were sluts, for lack of a better term, begging for a good-time fuck. The vampires were the worst. But Lily was smart and beautiful. Any well-respected vampire would be proud to bring her home to meet Mom. Except, whatever Lily was involved in, whomever she was involved *with*, she didn't want me to know about it, and I hoped she had a really good reason for not sharing.

At the end of the night, I left the club and headed home. I was in no mood to stay and mingle with a bunch of grabby women—vampire or human—I had no interest in.

The mansion was quiet when I entered via the back door. Even the help was gone. They only worked in the daytime while we slept, leaving Ari, our human confidante, to deal with them. I strolled through the kitchen, noticing that the dark, Italian marble floor gleamed from a recent buffing. Vicious, Chelle's puppy, came barreling through the opened double doors of the state-of-the-art kitchen and slid across the polished tile on her belly, nose-diving into my feet. Her long tail wagged with a soft thumping sound against the floor as her tongue lapped at my hands when I bent down to rub her tummy as she lay on her side. She was getting big.

"Hey, girl. What's ya doing? You lonely left here all by yourself?"

"She's not alone." My head jerked up at the sound of Chelle's voice. "Josh and I are here."

"Ah. Yes. Now I remember not seeing you at the club."

"What are you doing home so early?" she asked. Her multi-colored, short crop of hair stuck up as if she'd just been fucked, and I smiled and shrugged in response.

"Didn't feel much like partying tonight." I glanced at Josh, whose hair was just as messy. "Sorry if I interrupted you two." I patted Vicious on the back, indicating that she should get up because I was finished rubbing her tummy. Walking to the fridge, I reached in and grabbed a couple of bags of blood and handed one to Chelle.

"Thanks." She grinned and looked at Josh. "No worries. We're good. I was just coming in here for this." Chelle took the package and opened it, sucking the red liquid into her mouth.

Josh made a disgusted face and grabbed a beer from the fridge. "Anybody want one?"

"Yeah. I'll have one." I drained the rest of the blood from the plastic and threw the bag in the trash, then took the beer Josh held out for me. "Thanks, man."

I left the couple in the kitchen right after Josh sat on one of the chairs around the table and Chelle crawled up onto his lap. Not that it bothered me or anything, I just wanted some alone time. I had a feeling that the rest of the gang would be coming home soon, and I didn't want to be where I could be found. It never failed . . . as a family unit, when one of us was miserable, everyone wanted to help. And I didn't feel much like sharing my misery with that sort of bonding tonight.

I was still warm from the performance, so I shrugged off my jacket and shirt before walking out onto the veranda. The cool ocean breeze licked my nipples, and they hardened almost instantly from the chill. It was a clear night, and I could see all the way across the bay to the hills behind Tiburon. The city lights twinkled and the quarter moon sat high in the night sky surrounded by clusters of stars. My eyes widened at the sight of a shooting star. If I believed in fairytales, I'd have made a wish. Which made me think of Lily.

I polished off the last of the beer and headed back inside. Grabbing my shirt and jacket, I shrugged them back on and de-materialized.

I reappeared down in the Tenderloin district. I knew I was grasping at straws, but I wanted to see Lily so badly my chest hurt. I could only hope she'd come by. Unfortunately, there was no sign of Lily at The I.V., so I strolled down the street a short distance and thought about taking in some more nourishment. It had been a grueling, hot night on stage, and because I didn't know if I'd get to spend any time with Lily tonight, I was a bit depressed. Nothing like a little fresh blood to boost my spirits.

The only problem was, I didn't run across anyone who looked appetizing enough out there on the street. I stopped walking when I reached the front of an old movie theater. Why not? I went to the ticket booth and bought a ticket. I didn't even look to see what was playing. The theater was old and small, with only one screening room. Not like those giant, multiplex cinemas with fourteen or more screens boasting IMAX and 3D features these days.

I strolled down the aisle of the dark theater, passing row after row of vacant seats. The movie was already playing—the original *Star Wars*. There were a man and a woman sitting up front, but I didn't want to disturb them. Plus, they were too close to the screen, and I didn't want any witnesses from behind. I turned to look at the back of the theater again and saw her: a lone woman sitting in the back row, chomping on the contents of a bucket of popcorn. I headed toward her. The closer I got, I saw that she was about mid-forties with a pretty face, long red curls flowing over her shoulders. But I was only interested in her blood. Lily was still too much on my mind to want anything more. As I sat down next to the woman, she glanced over at me, concern igniting a spark behind her eyes, but I managed to capture her gaze with mine and held her attention as I smiled, silently willing her to like me. The silent compulsion flowed into her mind. I had a talent for compelling humans that way and it came in handy in places like these.

"Great movie," I whispered. "May I?" I asked, holding my hand over the bucket she held. When she nodded, I dipped my hand into her popcorn and grabbed a small handful. Tossing several kernels into my mouth, I chomped them down and then leaned into her, whispering close to her ear. "First time?"

"Huh?" She frowned and looked at me in question.

"The movie." I gestured toward the screen and inched a bit closer to her. "First time seeing this?"

She laughed. "Heavens, no. I saw this movie the day it came out. I was five years old. I've seen it at least twenty times since, maybe more."

"Ah." I nodded. "Me, too." I smiled and slipped my fingers into her shoulder-length, red hair, swishing it away from her neck. Her vein throbbed as she sat watching Han Solo switch the Millennium Falcon into hyperspeed.

"What's your name?"

"Judy."

"I'm going to taste you now Is that okay, Judy?"

"Yes. I would like that."

"I promise I won't hurt you."

"Okay. That's good."

Without further ado, I sank my fangs into her vein but froze after tasting her. This didn't feel right. My mind drifted to the beautiful whiskey laced eyes I wanted to be gazing into. I pulled back and gently slid my tongue over the small puncture wounds I'd made, not ingesting any more of her blood.

I sat back and sighed.

"Thanks, Judy. You won't remember any of this."

"Okay. And you're welcome." She smiled at me.

I picked up her hand and pressed my lips against her knuckles. "Again, thank you very much," I said as I stood and walked out of the theater, leaving her there, focusing on the movie.

I wished I knew where Lily was.

# CHAPTER 6

Lily

*D*aylight had begun to illuminate the sky, but the shades in my room at Dorian's high-rise building hadn't begun to close yet. This was just one of several buildings Dorian owned around the city and a few more were still under construction.

This grand suite took up the entire top level with hardwood floors throughout, expensive vintage area rugs strewn around the space, and soft, plush, dark red leather furniture in the living area. There were gorgeous views of the city from every room. He owned the entire building, and most of his minions had apartments of their own at various levels. My bedroom—yes, I had my own room; though at times it felt more like a prison—was done in dark, cherry wood with rich red drapes and a plush, velvet bedspread. It looked more like a whore's boudoir than a place for sleeping, but that was how Dorian wanted it. The theme was pretty consistent throughout the suite, though; most every room had the same type of décor.

"Dorian, didn't you change the time of the shades to daylight savings last night?"

He glanced at me for a brief second then back at the rolling, brass cart he'd had brought into my room for the evening. Picking up a decanter half filled with brandy, he poured the golden brown liquor into two dainty cordial glasses. When he didn't answer me, I added, "You know, spring ahead or fall back, depending on the season? This is fall. You should have adjusted the timer for the shades to close an hour earlier."

"Right. I'll get on that in a moment, my sweet, but first, I have a surprise for you." He wore black silk lounge pants and no shirt, showing off his chiseled chest and abs and smooth skin. The tattoo of a pocket watch covering his left breast reminded me of a warning that he might blow up as time ticked on. Though, I knew it was to represent the passage of his time on earth, which was, as far as I knew, several centuries by now. If he were a decent man, I'd almost find him sexy.

"Please, shut them now, Dorian," I begged. "I don't want to have to hide under the bed for the next hour, or wake to have all my energy drained from my body, rendering me helpless when the sun blares in here." He didn't seem to be concerned at all, and that worried me. For all I knew, he'd leave me in this room alone all day with the shades up and the sun blaring in.

"Fuck. You worry too much. But, okay." He strolled to the little electric timer switch on the wall by the door. Reaching into his pocket, he pulled out a small key and unlocked the lid, flipping it open. He placed his finger on one of the buttons and then shut and relocked the lid. The shades slid closed, and I sighed with relief. I hated that he locked that lid.

He was right that I worried. But it wasn't too much. He'd joked more than once about locking me in this room with the shades set to open before the sun went down, and I worried every morning that he would do it while I slept.

There were times that I couldn't leave the room. I'd tried several times to teleport out of there with no success. But then, other times, I had no problem. I didn't know what it was that Dorian did to my room, but I never asked about it. I was always too afraid that he'd think I wanted to run away from him and I didn't want to start that argument. The only reason I could think of for me not being able to dematerialize at certain times was that he'd had a wizard or witch put a spell on the room. Turning back toward the cart, he grabbed the two small glasses of brandy as he made his way toward me. He handed me one of the glasses, and I took it, sipped, and then set it down on the nightstand.

The fact that Dorian was spending extra time in my room tonight worried me. He'd never wanted me sexually, not completely. I wasn't the one he wanted. I knew that. *He* knew that, so his presence here had something to do with the surprise he'd mentioned. A surprise I had a bad feeling about. I picked up my glass again, putting it to my lips as I sipped.

"You said something about a surprise?" I asked, wanting to get it over with and not let the night turn into something else. He may not want to fuck me, but that never stopped him from wishing he did, and I didn't think I could endure another round of listening to him beat-off while he stared at my bare ass as he rubbed his free hand over it, fantasizing. The fact that he liked guys was no big secret to me or any other person in this household, and he knew he could get me to do practically anything as long as he held my brother captive.

"Ah. Yes." He clapped his hands twice, and the door flew open. Two seconds later, Julian stumbled in, instantly crumbling to his knees on the floor in front of Dorian.

"Julian!" I cried out and immediately set the brandy down and hurried to him, hugging his thin frame to mine. "Oh, Julian, are you okay?"

Of course he wasn't okay. He looked as if they'd been starving him of blood. His cheeks were sunken, and his eyes were dull. Dark circles shadowed both of his eyes. His clothes . . . I shook my head and sucked back a sob. He wore a skimpy pair of light blue boxer briefs that were so thin his skin showed through the flimsy material. The shirt he wore was as equally see-through. I had to get him out of there. Somehow, someway, before he ended up forgetting who he was or Dorian killed him. But the silver chain hanging around his neck and the silver fetters securing his wrists together not only kept him prisoner, they also kept me from removing them. The flesh around his neck and wrists was marred and singed from the burning of the silver.

I turned to Dorian. "Why are you doing this to him? Please, Dorian, let him go."

He laughed. "No way! He's my biggest moneymaker right now. Both the women and the men love him."

"He needs blood. Please, give him some blood," I begged.

"Go on." Dorian waved his arm in the air, and someone handed me a bag. I pressed the plastic to Julian's lips, and he sucked, looking up at me with gratitude. His eyes were so vacant, too empty. Was he drugged? I wasn't even sure if he knew who I was right then.

"Julian, I'm so sorry." I gently stroked my hand over his hair. Why are you treating him this way, Dorian? Why is he just staring into space as if he doesn't even see me? He can't make you any money if he's dead."

"Pffft. You and I both know he won't die from lack of blood. And it's not the silver that's making him so lethargic."

"Then what is it?"

"The silver's there to keep you from helping him. His gaze is blank from the Blaze I gave him."

"The Blaze?"

Dorian waved his hand in the air. "It's a harmless drug that makes him not care about things, that's all."

"It doesn't look harmless."

"It is. A friend came upon it recently through accidental discovery. When a small amount is injected into the vein of a vampire, their energy is drained. Similar to what the sun does without the lasting effect. But it only lasts a short while. Don't worry, he'll be back to normal in a few minutes."

"Well, he can't perform for you if he's too weak. Let him go. I'll take his place," I offered.

Dorian threw his glass across the room, and it shattered when it hit the wall. "You are not to be touched! You belong to me. No one lays a hand on you. Ever!" he shouted, his voice dipping into a dangerous tone. He'd never once had intercourse with me. He always pleasured himself, ejaculating while admiring my backside. Yet he claimed me as his.

With two wide steps, Dorian lifted me by my hair from my crouched position on the floor next to Julian. I cringed in agony. "I've told you many times, if anyone ever touches you, I will kill them. If anyone so much as looks at you with lust-filled interest, they will be sorry they ever laid eyes on you. Do you understand that, Lily? Do I make myself clear?"

I nodded as a tear escaped from my eye and ran down my cheek. I knew his threats well. I'd heard them before, and I always heeded them. Dorian scared me, and I never wanted to do anything that would make him punish me, though secretly meeting Preston has always been worth taking the chance. He eased his grip on my hair, moving his hand to the nape of my neck and covering my lips with his with so much force it hurt. Then he let go of me almost as forcefully, making me lose my balance. I fell to the floor on my ass beside Julian, who sat hunched in a ball, gulping the blood as if it were the first bag he'd had in a month.

Dorian's face softened as his finger skimmed my cheek. "You're a female, and I need you by my side when we are in public. No one is to touch you. You have a reputation to uphold. As for Julian, some of the bitches love him. Even some of the males want to be with him. He's so pretty." Dorian crouched down in front of Julian and lifted his chin so that Julian's lips were only an inch away from his, then he kissed him with passion, much more than he'd ever afforded me. I turned my head, not wanting to watch.

As I got up, Julian was being lifted up and dragged away out of the room, but he never made a sound. He'd been made into a sex slave as punishment for something he'd done years ago.

"You know he requires the hardening. Intimidation and deprivation of nourishment are the only things he responds well to," Dorian said, and as soon as we were once again alone, he slapped me so hard across the face that he knocked me completely back to the floor, my shoulder slamming against the hard surface.

"That's for shorting me on the drug money. Don't test me, Lily," he barked, taking a couple of steps toward the door before turning back and pointing his finger at me. "Don't short-change me again. You won't fair well."

Shit, I'd forgotten to find the money to add in before handing it over to Malik. Was that what this had all been about?

"I'm sorry, Dorian. I . . . those guys were short the cash, but they were regular customers. If I didn't sell the bag for less, I was afraid they'd find their junk somewhere else. We couldn't afford to lose them." I figured by adding in the "we," he'd take it as utter devotion.

His dark, dangerous eyes stared at me with contempt, then suddenly softened. He surprised me by saying, "Good call. But don't make deals like that again. I will be gone for several days. Do not, I repeat, *do not* do anything foolish." Then he left my room and shut the door. I heard the lock turn before his footsteps disappeared down the hallway. This was the first time in a very long while that he'd locked the door. That I knew of anyway. I sobbed into my hands. Why was this happening to my brother and me? Why did Dorian keep me?

But I knew why.

MUD SQUISHED under our shoes as we huddled against a building in the dark. As a carriage passed by, horse manure plopped to the puddle-riddled dirt road in front of us and splattered up onto our clothes. The delicate designs on the side of the conveyance, gave me the impression that the coach carried someone important and wealthy.

Once the carriage passed, I latched on to Julian's arm. "Come on. He has to be gone by now," he said.

The year was eighteen ninety-seven, and our clothes were in tatters—my dress torn and frayed at the bottom, Julian's pants in a similar condition from running through the unpaved streets of San Francisco.

We were the last of our family. Our father, Daniel Grey, had been taken from us by tuberculosis just the year before. Our mother, as well as our baby *sister, had died several years earlier during childbirth. Now, Julian and I were the only two left. At twenty, I was eleven months older than Julian, though he was six inches taller and much stronger.*

*After running for what seemed like hours, we headed home, positive the monster had moved on. As we entered our home, we knew we'd made a grave mistake. Julian shoved me behind him and I cringed at the shame that fell over me. I was supposed to be taking care of him. I was the eldest now.*

*Like a coward, I huddled behind my younger brother as the vampire loomed over us.*

# CHAPTER 7

The I.V. was dead—no pun intended. No soul but me and Sting—the bartender, not the singer—occupied the place. It was still early in the evening though, and I expected the small bar to fill up as the hours went by. The I.V. was one of several all-night bars in the city, but this one catered mostly to vampires. Though there was a straggler human once in a while. Whenever they'd venture in, all heads would turn at the scent. But there was no blood drinking allowed on the premises, so humans were safe if they came in. The rule kept the bar off the police's radar, though there was no telling what happened after said humans left. I'd been known to trace after a few ladies of the night that came in looking for business before. I wasn't above drinking from whores, though I preferred a more pure blood source. Not that all whores did drugs, but I'd venture a guess that the majority of them did; at least the ones who hung around The I.V. One sniff of that tainted blood, and I knew.

"I noticed you changed up your style a bit last week at Club Royal. You were good." Sting nodded, giving me a close-lipped grin of approval as he set my glass of scotch in front of me. Other than the spiky hair, nothing about this Sting resembled the famous singer. This

Sting had dark, almost black hair and dark eyes. I'd never seen him wear anything but white T-shirts and black Dockers.

"You were there?"

"Yep. I usually pop over there for a couple of hours to listen to you guys. Keeps my mundane life interesting. Everybody needs a little rock and roll. Helps keep the blood flowing." He chuckled.

I studied him for a minute. "Ever play?"

"Nah. Though I did manage the Stones for a couple of years."

"Hmmm . . . Ever hang with the Police?"

He chuckled.

"What's so funny?"

"Not the Police you're talking about."

"Oh." I smiled. "Then where'd you get your name?"

He laughed and scratched the tip of his ear with his finger. "I used to be known as "the stinger" back in the days of my human life. In the late eighteen hundreds, I led a series of sting operations, leading to the arrest of several famous criminals like Hoodoo Brown, the leader of the Dodge City Gang. Though that one never stuck."

"I remember hearing about that gang."

"Yep. His real name was Hyman G. Neill. It's rumored that he was shot and killed in a gambling dispute years later in Mexico."

"So, you were a cop?"

"U.S. Marshal."

I nodded my head with new respect for the vampire-turned-bartender. "How'd you turn?" I was fascinated now.

He grabbed the bottle of Johnny Walker and poured me another round. "Vegas was wild and lawless back then, riddled with thieves and murderers. And vampires. The railroad was new and easy prey for robberies. Jessie James was active, and a large sum of cash was being transported. Sixty grand to be exact. There were several of us marshals scattered around, staked out and waiting. A female vampire named Rita feigned being a damsel in distress and staggered through the brush as if she'd been thrown from her horse. Being the gentleman I was, I quickly dismounted to help her out. As soon as my feet touched the ground, she was on me, sinking her fangs into my neck. I honestly don't know what happened to the other five marshals who were part of that sting; I can only assume they were killed by Rita, though when I asked about them later on, she only shrugged and said I was in no position to press the matter. Later, when I awoke in her bedroom—I guess it was a few days later—she confessed that she couldn't kill me because she found me too attractive." He laughed and ran his palm over his mouth. "I have to admit, she was beautiful. I ended up staying with her and helped run a speakeasy in the early twentieth century. That's how I became a bartender."

"What happened to her?"

"She was beheaded by some vampire bootlegger who wanted to capitalize on the market. She was good to me, and it broke my heart. I went into hiding for about ten years after that. What about you, Elvis? What were you doing when you were turned?"

The door opened, and two young human men—clearly out of their element—entered.

Sting tapped his fist on the bar in front of me. "Another time."

I nodded.

The two men sat at the bar, a few stools away from me. They were dressed in jeans. One of them wore a black down jacket, while the other donned black leather. They each ordered a shot of whiskey. As Sting poured their drinks, a third guy walked in and sat next to them. He nodded at Sting and pointed at the glasses filled with amber liquid. Sting grabbed another tumbler and let the liquor flow into it. The third guy wore dark jeans and a black hooded sweatshirt.

I watched out of the corner of my eye as leather jacket guy pulled out a wad of money from his pocket, keeping it low under the bar. Hooded sweatshirt guy quickly snatched it up, exchanging it for a bag full of white powder that I assumed was heroin or meth. Maybe cocaine. I hated all that shit. After the exchange, hooded sweatshirt guy drank his drink and then got up and left. The two remaining punks drained their glasses and got up, as well. One of them placed a twenty-dollar bill on the bar. "Will that cover all three drinks?" he asked Sting.

"That'll do it. You boys stay safe, now."

When the door closed behind them, I made a small *tsk* sound and shook my head. "Slam bam thank you, ma'am. You do know they just used your place for a drug buy, right?"

Sting shrugged. "Heroin. Sometimes meth. It used to bother me. I complained to the local PD once years ago, and the very next day, I found my bike smashed to holy hell in the parking lot of my apartment building with a note attached to it. It said, *Try interfering with my business again, and next time it will be your head. Only it won't be smashed, vampire, it will be severed.* I did some asking around and found out that the guy who runs the drugs not only has strong ties to the cartel in Mexico, but he's also a very old and powerful vampire. My law enforcement days are long gone, and I like my head where it is. So I've learned to turn a blind eye."

"That guy that was just in here wasn't a vampire."

"No. He's very much a human. A human controlled by a vampire. One I don't want to be on the bad side of."

I nodded. What the hell did I care? If humans wanted to destroy their bodies with heroin, who was I to mind? Only thing I cared about was the blood I drank. If it was tainted with drugs, it tasted nasty.

Sting poured me another glass of JW. "You've been coming in here for several months now. Is that the first time you noticed the drug deals?"

"Yeah. I guess." Most of the time, my eyes were on Lily.

"Well, take my advice. Pretend you didn't see it. You don't want to mess with that group. I'd hate to see you lose your head."

# CHAPTER 8

orian left me secured in my room and never came back before he left, leaving me locked up the entire time he was gone. Malik brought me my daily doses of blood—always Malik since Jace, Dorian's other servile, had most likely gone on the trip with him.

I paced the room, waiting for the shades to go up, indicating that it was finally nighttime. Or, at least dark outside. I needed to get out of there. Not only because I was going stir-crazy, but I needed to see Preston. I could only imagine what must be going through his mind regarding why I hadn't been around to see him.

My feet hurt from wearing five-inch high-heeled boots all day, waiting for Malik to bring me blood. I needed the height of the heels to do what needed to be done since Malik was at least six-foot-two to my five-eight.

The door handle turned, and Malik stepped into the room, carrying a tray with two bags of blood and a glass.

"I'm famished. What took you so long?" I asked with a great amount of desperation in my voice as I stepped closer to him, feigning starvation.

"Sorry, love. Couldn't be helped. There were several new turnouts

47

that came in, and few needed some extra tending to. With Jace and Dorian gone, it took extra time."

"Turnouts?" I'd heard the term before while eavesdropping on one of Dorian's conversations.

"Ahhh. You know. The new prostitutes. We had a couple reckless eyeballers who couldn't keep their peepers on the ground. Dorian would be as pissed off as yellow snow if one of them had to 'choose up' by mistake next week when he takes them to market." Choosing up was a bad thing from what I understood. If one of the prostitutes made eye contact with another pimp—accidentally or on purpose—it meant they were choosing him as their new handler. And if the original pimp wanted that prostitute back, he'd have to pay a fee to the new guy. "Then, after that bit of training," Malik continued, "we had to brand them. And you know that takes a while."

My hand immediately went to the right side of my neck to the small tattoo Dorian had insisted my brother and I get years ago. It was a branding. He owned us.

Dorian hadn't always exploited humans—or vampires. It was something he'd just started recently. I hadn't realized the enterprise had gotten so expansive, or that he was dealing on such a large scale.

"Why do you look so surprised? You know Dorian supplies some of the best young men and women on this circuit for trade and sale."

I nodded, but in truth, I hadn't realized things had grown so much. I knew he exploited Julian and the occasional female prostitute, but nothing like what Malik had just described. I knew from various social gatherings and parties that I'd attended alongside Dorian that he was considered one of the most prominent and influential businessmen in San Francisco. But using that legitimate hotel business as a cover for his human trafficking scam seemed a bit risky, even for Dorian.

I was losing my nerve, but I needed to get out. As Malik bent over to place the tray on the small table by the wall, I stepped up behind him. "I'm sorry, Malik. I'll be back soon." I said, placing my hands on either side of his head and snapping his neck, rendering him helpless.

He appeared to be dead. But I knew he would survive. He'd be super pissed off at me when he woke, but he would be fine. I knew he'd never voluntarily let me go out without permission, but I had to trust that he wouldn't rat me out to Dorian. I thought Malik and I were close. We'd had each other's backs on more than one occasion.

I shrugged into my coat and stepped out of the room, de-materializing outside the back door to The I.V. The first person I saw when I entered the bar brought an elated feeling to my soul. Preston looked up at me and greeted me with the most delicious smile I'd ever seen—a look I hadn't even realized I needed. I looked around the room to make sure no one I knew was in there. Satisfied that I didn't know any of the patrons I saw, I hurried to Press, and he caught me in his arms. He smelled delicious—like apples and honey mixed with hickory smoked wood.

I looked around the room again and then up at him. Swallowing the lump in my throat that the fear in my bones caused, I asked, "Can we go somewhere else? Somewhere warm?" I added, not wanting to be on top of the old lighthouse platform.

Without any question, he reached into his pocket and pulled out a twenty, threw it down on the bar, and took hold of my hand. He waved to the bartender and ushered me out the back door, then pulled me against him. "Hold on."

We rematerialized inside what I assumed was his bedroom. I had no idea where he lived, but this room had just about everything anyone could ever want.

He strolled to the door and closed and locked it before flipping a switch on the wall, softly illuminating the entire room, the lights glowing with a soft blue ambiance.

"Make yourself at home."

He didn't need to ask me twice as I pulled off the very uncomfortable high-heeled boots I'd had on way too long and sank my toes into a plush, light tan area rug covering the dark wood flooring beneath a king-size bed. Preston headed to a small bar area and poured us a couple of drinks as I gave myself a quick tour.

On the other side of the room, directly in front of the bed, was a soft brown leather sofa facing a large screen TV that hung on a blue wall above a stone fireplace. The other door in the room was a bathroom, and I peeked in to see a wide spa tub encircled by a bed of small, round stones. It too was drenched in blue light, floating down from above it. The shower was wide and open with a rain-shower sprayer at each end and multiple other showerheads across the ceiling.

Press handed me a tumbler of something golden brown and I sniffed. Whiskey.

"I love this suite. Did you decorate it?"

He grinned. "Yes. And I hired someone. Come, let's sit."

I followed him to another sofa. This one was cream-colored and soft and plush, though it had no backing, just high, comfy-looking side arms graced with several small pillows of different shades of blue. I was beginning to get the distinct feeling that blue was Preston's favorite color, or maybe it was just because it all went together so well. We sat facing a large picture window all drenched in blue light beaming down from the ceiling, giving way to a gorgeous view of the Golden Gate Bridge and the city lights of Tiburon across the bay. I couldn't help but stare at the way the blue light changed the coloring of my hands and Preston's face. It was very easy on the eyes, as well as romantic.

Press took a sip of his drink then set the glass down on the table beside him. "I was holding off asking what's so important that you needed privacy, hoping you'd decide to start talking, but it seems you are either too wrapped up in my furnishings, or you're scared to tell me. I'm guessing it's the latter."

He gently grabbed my hand, took the drink from my other one, and set it down, urging me closer to him. As I gazed into his dark eyes, a golden glow growing in them, I had a sad thought that this might be the last time I ever got a chance to be with him. Taking a chance like this was just too dangerous and I never knew when Dorian or his watchdogs would discover my whereabouts. But here we were now, alone in a bedroom made for romance and this was an opportunity I shouldn't waste.

I'd spent too many years being afraid of the consequences of my actions and there was no one I'd rather defy Dorian with than Preston.

"I don't want to talk," I said and leaned in to kiss him. He didn't miss a beat and wrapped his arms around me, pulling me closer. He took over, and as my lips parted, welcoming him, he slipped his tongue in. Taking me, possessing me the way I wanted to be possessed. With affection, desire, and an undertone of urgency neither of us could deny. I didn't feel owned or branded as someone's belonging with Preston. I didn't feel as if I were with him out of obligation to protect someone else. I just enjoyed him . . . *this* to the fullest. Every touch, every kiss was new. The sensations he brought to life inside of me made me realize what it felt like to live. Preston made me feel alive again. The realization, the feeling of being fully desired took over completely, and I clenched my legs together as heat gathered at my core.

"Are you sure, Lily?" Preston broke the kiss to ask as he trailed small, quick kisses down my neck and over the tops of my breasts.

"Yes. I've never been more sure about anything in my life."

"I've needed to touch you for so long. I'm not sure I *could* stop now."

His mouth caressed mine again; his tongue sliding over my lips in a sensual glide before slipping into my mouth. His kiss sent scorching heat through my veins. His hand roamed my thigh and moved up. The beat of my heart quickened and pounded against my chest. Or was that his? Maybe it was both. Two hearts beating as one.

When his fingers slipped beneath my skirt and inside my panties, I gasped at the unexpected pleasure as his forefinger found my clit, and I bucked my hips a little toward him for more. I couldn't get enough. I startled at the sensation of my fangs elongating. A sexual stimulation I'd never experienced before. I caught sight of Preston's face. He smiled, showing me his fangs. We were instantly on our feet, and it was suddenly so warm.

51

"Too many clothes," I huffed out as I struggled with his shirt, and he unzipped my skirt, letting it fall to the floor. He shrugged out of his shirt, and I splayed my hands over his taut chest. His muscles were so defined. He pulled my top over my head. I had no bra. I never wore one. Even though I was over a hundred years old, my breasts were exactly the same as they had been when I was twenty, the age I was when Dorian changed both my brother and me.

The frenzy stopped for a minute, and Preston gathered me in his arms, cradling me with tenderness as he walked us over to the large bed covered with a puffy, midnight-blue down comforter. When he laid me across the bed, I sank down several inches into the covers, and I felt like I was floating on a cloud. I laughed. He took hold of my hands and pulled me to stand once more at the edge of the bed as he squatted in front of me, tugging my panties down to the floor. Lifting my foot up to his lips, he kissed the inside of my ankle and continued pressing little kisses all the way up the inside of my leg until he reached my core. Then his fingers dipped inside my folds.

"Lily, you're so wet already." He smiled and slid his tongue from my opening to my clit. Stopping at the very top, he sucked and flicked his tongue over my nub as his finger slipped inside, and his thumb took over pleasuring where his tongue had been. "And so tight." He sank his fangs into my thigh very close to my opening, right at the crease of my leg and my folds. He suckled and drank and made little circles against my clit with his thumb as he sank another finger inside, pressing.

Releasing.

Squeezing.

Gently.

Hard.

Rubbing until I shuddered uncontrollably.

I let out a loud moan as my thoughts exploded inside my mind as he drank from me. I couldn't wait to do the same thing to him. He switched from sucking at my thigh to my folds, licking the length of my core and sucking at the nub that throbbed for his attention. Giving me everything I needed, he alternated back and forth between my mound and the crease of my leg. I shuddered, delirious with excitement, and it got to the point where I couldn't tell where his mouth was.

Preston took me to another world that I never wanted to return from. When he'd had his fill, he gently licked the small punctures closed. He shoved his pants down as I sat on the bed and watched him reveal himself, and then I leaned back on my elbows as he sauntered to me. He kissed his way up my stomach until he reached my neck, and I thought he would bite me again at that vein. Instead, he covered my mouth with his and urged me higher on the bed. My legs naturally accommodated his sexy frame as his weight pressed into me. And then, he sank into me. I gasped at the twinge of pain brought on by his thickness as he entered. The sudden discomfort took me by surprise. I hadn't expected the pinch.

Then he stopped all movement. His eyes locked on mine.

"Lily. You were a virgin? You didn't tell me. I'm sorry, I didn't know. Are you okay?"

"Yes." I could barely utter the word, my breath was so ragged with need. But he stayed still, waiting for an explanation. The guilt coating his eyes gave me pause and the strength to speak. "Don't be sorry. How could you know? I'm sure it's not often that you run across a hundred-and-twenty-year-old virgin. But an innocent no longer." I smiled and raised my head to kiss him, brushing a few strands of my hair out of the way.

"What is this?" Preston asked, touching the small tattoo that Dorian had insisted Julian and I get.

"It's nothing, just a silly tattoo I got years ago. It's supposed to be a present, a gift," I said, keeping the real meaning of the ink to myself. Though I hadn't lied. It *was* a gift box with a D in the middle of it. Dorian had been so delighted about Julian and I having the tiny gift boxes with his initial inked at our veins since the origin of his name, Doron, was Greek meaning *gift*.

"A gift to your vein?" he asked and smiled as he placed a small kiss by the tattoo. And then he met my lips with an urgent yet tender kiss before turning his head and offering me his vein.

I didn't hesitate and sank my fangs deeply into the side of his neck. The rush of his blood into my system set off an uncontrollable and pleasurable delirium deep within me. A tsunami of pleasure exploded within, and I cursed Dorian for putting so much fear in me all these years. The fear that he'd discover my disobedience if I ever lost my virginity.

# CHAPTER 9

Preston

*I* should have known the moment I sank my fangs into her delicious, soft skin next to her core that she was a virgin. Her blood was so rich, so potent, so much like a human's . . . But I'd gotten high on the sensation so quickly, the notion had left my brain almost as soon as it entered. She was right, of course. Who would have ever thought she would be a virgin? Running across a vampire who was a virgin was unheard of.

As I sank deep into her tight sheath, her moans of pleasure grew louder, and she moved her hips under me. The pleasure of her draw on my vein made me frenzied, and I needed to go deeper, the tight- ness of her walls only making the sensation stronger. I'd never been with a virgin before.

I rolled us over so her body was on top of mine. She continued to suckle at my vein, the power of the rush almost too much. Pushing myself up, I grabbed on to her hips and positioned her on my lap as my cock sank deeper inside. She released her grip on my vein and licked the small wounds she'd created, sealing them with a delicate swipe of her tongue. Her head straightened. We locked eyes. Hers heavy-lidded and sultry, a golden glow in them I hadn't noticed before. A color similar to mine when aroused—or so I'd been told. A color I hadn't seen in years.

I lost that thought, consumed by the pleasure of her movements. Lily rode me, taking all of me inside. I helped her move with my hands, gyrating her, pumping her against my cock, her walls contracting around me. With each movement, I felt myself change. I would never be the same again. Not after experiencing this with Lily.

With my hands on her ass, she rocked on top of me. Riding me like she knew what she was doing. The motion was so tantalizing, I couldn't hold back much longer. Her beautiful eyes found mine as her breath hitched and she came with a moan, just as I exploded into her sweetness.

I PULLED LILY against me so that her head rested on my chest, our bodies stretched out side by side. I loved the feel of her skin against mine, so soft, like the petals of a rose. Or a lily. I'd always loved their soft, fragrant, trumpet-shaped petals. I snuggled her closer to me, wanting her to be a part of me. An extension. One where I ended and Lily began. As if our souls fused together as one.

I knew there was something troubling her, and I wanted her to tell me what it was. I also wanted to know how—and why—she had remained a virgin all these years. But I wouldn't push.

I took a deep breath, and her head moved up with my chest and then down again when I exhaled. She giggled and lifted her head so she could look at my face. She was so beautiful with her hair all messed up from my fingers tangling in it while we made love.

When she lay back down, I sighed again, only not quite as prominently. She took my hand, twisting her fingers with mine.

"I'm sure you want answers," she said as she traced her finger up and down the inside of my thigh all the way from my knee to my sack.

It tickled, but felt amazing at the same time, and I never wanted her to stop.

"I do. But only if you want to tell me." I wasn't going to pry into her past or her present if she didn't want me there. But I hoped she did. I wanted her to let me in and allow me to take her away from everything that tormented her. I had demons that plagued me, as well. I was sure most vampires did. So I knew that whatever was bothering her couldn't be anything that would shock me.

"I want to tell you. But not tonight. Let's just enjoy this moment and not taint it with unnecessary swill."

"Swill?" I chuckled and frowned, giving her an I-don't-believe-you-just-used-wet-pig-feed-to-describe-your-life look. "You didn't by any chance grow up on a farm, did you?"

"I did." She laughed.

"My little farm girl." I kissed the top of her head.

"My father liked to joke that we had the largest farm of any twenty miles due west. We had the far west spread, and there wasn't another plot of land like ours until the next town over, which was about twenty miles away." Her laughter was music to my ears.

"Why did you leave the farm?" I asked.

Then she became somber, quiet even. I waited, hoping she'd tell me a little more about herself. Her voice was soft as she spoke.

"Both our parents were gone. Tuberculosis took my father. My mother had died several years earlier giving childbirth. Julian and I were the only ones left. We were young and naïve. I was only twenty and he was nineteen. We couldn't work the farm on our own after our father's passing, so we sold it and took what little money we got from the sale to go and live in the city where we thought life would be easier. Julian had his paper routes and helped out at the corner drug store sweeping, cleaning, and a variety of other duties. I tried to learn to sew to help bring in more money, but I had two thumbs when it came to directing a needle—or so my mother had said—so I sought work outside the home, cleaning others' residences. When Julian and I returned home after our respective jobs that fateful day, we found our next door neighbor's apartment open and the door torn from the hinges. Inside, we discovered her body. Her neck torn to shreds by some horrible monster. We thought the creature may have still been there. So we ran away.

"But he found you?"

"Not exactly. We returned home after hours of running with the thought that he surely had to have moved on by then."

"But he hadn't."

"No. He turned my brother first. I don't remember much about it." She turned to snuggle tighter against me. "Where did you grow up?" she asked.

The abrupt change of subject startled me and I gave her a side-long glance. Her eyes glimmered with the soft blue light that trickled down from the ceiling. Was I ready to tell her my story? She'd given me a small glimpse of herself. I needed to give her a piece of me. The problem was, I wanted to give her *all* of me, and I wanted to take all of her. I wanted to know everything about her, but I knew she wasn't ready. However, if I gave her as much of me as I could, maybe she would give me a bit of herself in return.

"My mother was a drug addict and died in my arms when I was five," I supplied rather nonchalantly, even for me. I'd wanted the statement to come across as if the experience weren't any big deal, but Lily's body tensed against mine nonetheless. "I was born premature, though back then, they weren't really sure. Since my mother was a prostitute, she had no idea who my father was, or even how long she'd been pregnant before she knew for sure. I had a very low birth weight, as well as breathing issues, and I was born with a deformed left leg and foot. I wore a leg brace my entire life. I couldn't get across the room without the aid of a crutch." Lily looked down at my feet, and I wiggled my now perfect toes. "Becoming a vampire healed all of my deformities," I added. "With all those issues, no one wanted to take me in after my mother's death, so I ended up in an orphanage until I was eighteen."

"I'm sorry, Preston. You must have had a very difficult childhood."

"It was what it was. I don't talk about it often. Well . . . never. I guess you could say my childhood gave me a great distaste for drug users, and I don't like to drink from prostitutes, which somewhat limits my fresh blood intake." Lily's body stiffened against mine, and I wondered if she felt sorry for me or hated drugs too. She had secrets she hadn't divulged yet, but I wouldn't judge. I liked her too much to ridicule any of the choices she'd made, and being the kind and sensitive person I knew her as, I was positive that most of those—whatever they were—had to be for a great reason. It took a lot of courage and effort to get through a hundred plus years on earth and all the fucked up baggage that came with it. We'd both been in this messed up world for a long time. There would be no asshole judgments coming from me.

"When did you get turned?"

"I was nineteen years old. After I left the orphanage, I had trouble finding work because of my illness, the constant asthma very prevalent and noticeable. No one wanted to hire me. I was weak and could barely lift a twenty-pound sack without coughing. Not to mention the issues with my leg."

Her eyes widened, and she sat up and stared at me. "I'm older than you?" The surprised expression on her face ignited her dark eyes with an amber glow once more. The same way they had looked when she climaxed while I'd taken blood from her thigh. I imagine they had again later, as well, but I couldn't see her face then since her mouth had been buried against my neck, and then later, I had come with her, and my mind was elsewhere.

"You are." I laughed. "Don't worry. I've always liked older women." I winked and tucked her closer against me.

"I did land a job as a school teacher, though it had its share of challenges. It took time to charm my way into each kid's heart in order to get them to look past my disabilities and want to respect my authority without their ridicule. I'd spent a lot of time as a kid playing the piano in the home I lived in. No one wanted much to do with me, so I sat in front of those ivory keys day after day and taught myself how to play. I discovered that through music and my love of songwriting, I could get them all to learn while having fun doing it.

"As for my transformation . . . I'd worked late that night grading papers and hadn't noticed the huge storm brewing outside. Thinking back, it had to have been a hurricane, but back then they didn't have machines to calculate the speed of the wind, nor was there any way to send out a warning. I was on my way home—I rented a room at Mrs. Johnson's boarding house in town, so I didn't have all that far to go—but the storm was intensifying.

"Initially, when I stepped outside the school house, I almost turned back and stayed inside. But I needed to get a good night's sleep since I'd been up late the night before writing a song—something I did for fun. So, I braved the storm and clutched my satchel full of books and papers close against my chest. But the heavy gusts of wind stole it from my grasp almost immediately. I couldn't even see which direction it flew, so I ignored it and hurried along as fast as I could, which wasn't very fast with the leg brace I still wore. My leg never did improve. In fact, it got harder and harder to move as I grew older."

I looked down at Lily. Her finger still moved gently over my leg, so I knew I hadn't lost her to sleep yet, but being sympathetic, knowing how long-winded I could be once I had someone's attention, I asked. "Am I boring you yet?"

"No! Absolutely not. I find your story captivating. Please, go on."

I sucked in a breath and sat up. Placing my hands around Lily and bringing her with me, I lifted her up and then set her back down so her legs straddled mine. I wanted to look at her. I wanted her to see me. Her dark eyes gleamed with empathy, and her lips were still plump from my kisses and stained red with my blood. The empathy I didn't fully understand. How could she comprehend the magnitude of my illness?

Now that she was in this pose, my cock hardened, and I wanted her again. My hand rose as if of its own accord and caressed the nape of her neck. I gently pulled her close, pressing my lips against hers, tasting my blood still lingering on her tongue. I placed my hands under her, raising her up to position her back down over me as her wetness coated my erection. When she pulled her hair to the side, revealing the vein that throbbed, I took it. Taking turns, we shared each other as she moved on top of me. Our blood would be forever mixed. The magnitude of our orgasms exploding together exceeding every sexual experience I'd ever had.

We held each other after, our breaths labored. We stayed that way until our breathing normalized once again. Lily spoke first.

"You're amazing. A sex god."

I laughed. "And how would you know?" The moment the words left my lips, I wanted to take them back. Her face became somber, and I badly wanted to wipe that look of gloominess away. There was so much more to Lily than I ever thought possible. With far more tact than I had just demonstrated, I would find out everything about her.

"I read a lot." She laughed, and I was relieved that she hadn't taken offense to my rudeness.

"Ah, romance novels no doubt. Or do you indulge in erotica?"

"Mostly just steamy romance, though some erotica, I guess." Her voice turned shy with the confession, and I loved it. "Finish telling me about how you became a vampire."

I left her sitting on top of me with her legs straddling mine. I needed to watch her eyes and her lips as I spoke.

"Where was I?"

"You had just left the school house, and there was a storm. By the way, it was rather mean of you to distract me from such a riveting story that way."

"Are you complaining?"

"No." She gave me a sweet smile. "It was worth it."

Every facet of Lily delighted my senses. She could say or do no wrong in my eyes.

"Well, when I left the school, I made my way through the trees, and a loud crack reverberated through the air, followed by a sound resembling an explosion. I turned to look in the direction of the boom as a large tree trunk headed right towards me. As I stood watching the tree plummet in my direction, frozen in place and unable to move, knowing it could be my end, someone came out of nowhere and grabbed me, whisking me away so fast I couldn't see who they were or where we were going. When he placed me on my feet somewhere several miles away, I immediately threw up into some bushes. Out of the corner of my eye, I saw a large man standing by, observing me as I retched into a row of hedges that lined the walkway where we stood. When I finished losing everything except my guts, I looked up to see a small cottage. The wind was still strong and threatening as he tugged me inside. He asked when I'd last eaten, and I told him not since that morning. He told me to sit by the fire and gave me some broth and brandy. I sipped at both as he watched. I asked him how we'd managed to get to the house so fast, but he only shrugged and said, "I will tell you in due time. For now, drink. You'll need your strength."

After I had finished both the broth and brandy, I thanked him. He'd saved my life. I offered him money, but he didn't want any monetary compensation."

"What did he want?" I heard the trepidation in her voice as she asked so quietly.

"He wanted a companion."

"What kind of companion?"

"I think you know."

She nodded.

"He told me he could fix my body. I laughed, coughing as I always did from the asthma. When he told me he was a vampire, I scoffed at him. Disbelieving. But I knew deep down that he spoke the truth from the speedy way in which we'd flown through the air. I'd heard rumors of such creatures, those who defied death. Death as I'd known it at the time anyway. Immortal beings, demons from hell. But he didn't seem like a demon to me. Besides, I told myself if he had wanted to harm me, he would have already, and he wouldn't have saved me from the falling tree."

"So you let him turn you?"

"Yep. I've never looked back since."

"You like being a vampire?"

"Shit, yeah."

"But what about the companion part? Did you love him?" Her question wasn't an accusation. It was simply an inquiry filled with curiosity.

"I grew to love him. Yes." Her gaze darted to her hands in her lap as she twisted her fingers. A nervous habit I'd noticed from earlier. I knew the question of my sexual orientation must be looming at the front of her mind, and it seemed to bother her.

"But not in the way he wanted. I'm not gay, Lily."

"I think we've established that." She smiled sweetly. "But why did you stay with him?"

"Because I *did* care for him. He made me whole. He saved me from a hardship I never thought I'd escape from. I gave him whatever he wanted."

"Including sex?" she asked.

"Yes. In exchange, he provided for me, showed me what I needed to do to survive the new life he'd given me." I laughed at a memory. "There were a few occasions when we'd go out hunting and he'd insist on bringing home a female for me to enjoy. I'm not bi-sexual and he knew I preferred women, and he wanted to make sure I was taken care of in that way."

"If you aren't bi-sexual and you're definitely not gay, that must have been difficult to allow him to do what he did with you."

"It was, but I was so grateful for the life he'd given me, and I'd made the deal with him. I felt obligated to honor it. I'd have given anything to no longer be trapped in that body. I'm not making excuses for being with him," I added, though I realized that was exactly what I was doing as guilt swamped me for wanting the life he'd given me in exchange for sex. The thought of using my body as payment for something like eternal life hadn't bothered me in the slightest back then.

"Lily, I'd had a shitty, difficult childhood. Living with disease was extremely hard, especially during that era. When someone came along and offered me an illness-free eternal life? You bet your beautiful, sexy derrière I took it."

I stopped talking when she became placid, and I sat up and tilted her chin up with my finger so that her eyes were level with mine.

"Do you still love him?" I had known that question was coming.

"In a way, yes. But never in the way he wanted me to love him. But he's gone now."

"Where?"

"I don't know. I kept my position at the school for several years, making excuses about finding a miracle worker of a doctor who was just passing through town, until it got to the point where I thought people had begun to notice that I hadn't aged. One day, I came home from school, and he was gone. Just like that. He left me a note, saying that he was thankful for my companionship but that he needed to move on."

I paused for a few seconds, remembering how lost I'd been and how empty I'd felt inside being left alone without the companionship of another vampire. "I knew it was more than that. I couldn't hide the fact that I liked being with women more than him. He knew I craved the love and touch of a female. I just grew to love him because of who he was and what he'd done for me."

"Then it seems as if he took advantage of you. Maybe even abused you."

"You can think of it that way if you want to, and I suppose you might be right in a way. I've never taken another male lover since my sire, nor have I ever told anyone this. Not even my best friend, Gage. It's not exactly a conversation I want to have with any of my band-mates. I doubt they'd make fun of me, but I never wanted to give them the opportunity. And it's *usually* not very good bedroom conversation."

I smiled and flipped her onto her back as I climbed on top of her in a playful way, kissing her neck and sliding my tongue down to the tips of her breasts.

"But you told me."

Lifting my head, I glanced at her. "Yes. I want you to know everything about me. I care about you. I care *for* you. You must know that." I kissed her nipple and then playfully nipped at it.

She remained quiet. Docile even.

"What is it, love? Why are you so sad all of a sudden? You don't like being a vampire do you?"

"It's not that I don't like it . . ."

"What, then? Tell me."

# CHAPTER 10

Lily

"It's late. I should be going."

I wiggled out from under Preston and found all my clothes that had been strewn around the room. Lying there with him had been wonderful. *He* was wonderful. His story was enthralling, and I wanted so much to be like him. I wanted to embrace my vampirism. But I couldn't. I was a vampire owned by another, and I couldn't find a way out. The idea of Press loving a man didn't bother me. I understood that kind of love. Especially with one's sire. In a way, I loved Dorian, but over the years, that love had turned to hatred as my freedom turned to captivity. Preston's story should have made my confessions easier. But it didn't.

"Lily, wait. It's still early. It's only five in the morning. Can't you stay a little while longer? The sun won't be up for another hour and a half. I'll take you home myself."

Wouldn't that be something? To have Preston take me home.

Home to Dorian. Preston had no idea what kind of life I led. He hated drugs and prostitutes. Had said as much. His mother had died in his arms from a drug overdose, and her prostitution had created him. How would he take it when I told him that I had to peddle heroin every night? Or that I lived with a man who pimped prostitutes and sold women and men into sex slavery. There was no way I could reveal where I lived, whom I lived with. Preston would hate me. He would never understand.

Tonight had been nothing but the realization of the dream I'd wanted. That was all. I had gotten exactly what I wanted. Now, I could move on. Forget Preston.

"I'm sorry, Preston. I really need to go."

I finished pulling on my boots and headed toward the door. Preston quickly tugged up his pants and followed me out. When I entered the hallway, I stopped when I heard voices. People stood around, talking. His bandmates. Their women. They were all there, and they all stopped talking and stared at me when I stumbled into view. Preston came and stood beside me, barefooted, his pants zipped but not buttoned, showing a bit of the hair that I had just run my fingers through. He wore no shirt, and his hair was messed and tangled as I'm sure my own locks were with that just-fucked appearance. He looked delicious, and I wished I didn't have to leave him.

"Elvis!" one of them said in a surprised voice, using that ridiculous nickname. Preston stood silently beside me, and they all just kept staring as if they'd never seen another vampire before. Well, maybe not one coming from Preston's room with messed-up hair and a satiated glow that I was sure I had. If vampires could blush, I was sure my cheeks would be a deep, dark shade of pink. "Are you going to introduce us?"

"Oh, yeah," Preston began. "This is Lily, my girlfriend." The new title gave me goosebumps. I hadn't been prepared for it. I'd wanted it, but I knew it could never be. I hated that I was the only one who knew that this had just been a one-night stand.

"Hi, I'm Maggie, and this is Cian." A petite young woman and a male vampire that I recognized approached me. She draped her arm around his waist as she held out her hand to me. I shook it. She was small, a few inches shorter than me. Her beautiful, dark locks were pulled back and secured into a ponytail. Tight, cropped workout pants displayed her shapely figure. Now that I looked closer, they were all dressed as though they'd just returned from the gym.

I took Cian's hand when he reached out to claim mine. He was handsome, with a neat, short haircut. His smile, as well as his grip, were welcoming.

Another male stepped toward me. "Hi, I'm Gage. I'm Elvis's best friend," he said with pride, and I instantly liked him. He took my hand and held it, the movement slight but strong. Gage was taller than Preston. In fact, he was taller than all of them. His unruly light brown curls fell loosely to his shoulders, and his smile was infectious.

"I'm Lane, and this is V." Lane was even more handsome up close than on stage. I knew he and Cian were twins, but the resemblance was only slight. They were both fine-looking vampires, but Lane, like my brother, was pretty . . . only with an air of playfulness and danger. A joviality that Julian had possessed at one time until Dorian's dangerous drug had claimed him, stealing the goodness and strength that made my brother the man he'd grown to be.

"Short for Vanessa." The female vamp smiled and held out her hand. She was tall, like me, and her two long, golden, pink tipped braids flowed down over the straps of the pink jog bra she wore. My senses flared when our grasps met. She was different from anyone I'd ever come in contact with before. As if she sensed my discomfort, she said, "I'm a witch." It wasn't until then that I noticed the crystal hanging around her neck. But then she smiled, showing fangs, and I stumbled back a little. I'd never encountered a vampire witch before. "I know, it's a rarity. But it happens." She shrugged and smiled, and I returned the sentiment.

A large human male walked up behind them.

"That's Ari," Preston supplied.

"Hi-ya." He raised his hand in a wave. He didn't seem frightened.

Perhaps he was compelled. But I recognized him from the club. He was one of the bouncers there. It had always struck me as strange that a club frequented mostly by vampires had a human for a bouncer. But no one ever seemed to be bothered by it.

"What's going on? Why's everybody congregating in the hallway?" A pretty young woman with short, blue-and-red-streaked hair chased an adorable chocolate brown Labrador puppy down the hallway. Another human guy trailed behind them. "Oh. Hi," she said, stopping when she reached the group, but the dog simply continued padding its way to me, wagging its tail very fast. I liked dogs. Always had, and this one was a little irresistible, so I bent down and gave her some love behind her ears and on her tummy when she flopped down on her back at my feet.

"This is Lily. Lily, that's Chelle and Josh." Preston gestured to the couple. "And this is Vicious." Preston looked down at the bundle of joy I was petting. I smiled at the ironic name for the delightful creature.

Getting back to my feet, I noticed that everyone stood around grinning. They were all just so . . . there, smiling as though they all liked one another. No, not just liked, supported. Maybe even loved. No one seemed to be worried about a stranger among them. I suddenly felt out of place. This was all foreign to me. I needed to leave. I hadn't counted on meeting anyone, and especially not everyone. I wasn't ready. I hadn't been mentally prepared.

"Nice to meet you all," I managed to say and gave them all a tight smile. "I'm sorry. I was just leaving."

"I'll walk you out," Preston said and placed his hand on the small of my back, leading me away from the group.

"Bye. Come back soon," I heard one of the guys call out.

They were a family. I could sense the closeness, the love emanating from them and suffusing the air. It had been years since I'd witnessed anything like that. Not since . . . I didn't want to think about that. That was another life. But I was sensitive to those emotions. I always had been, even when I was human. I wasn't psychic, just susceptible to the feelings and attitudes of others. As a child, making friends had always been difficult as their feelings seemed to get in the way of my own.

Maybe that was why I'd always hung out with my brother. His emotions were so similar to my own. My mother always told me I let people get to me more than I should. She'd never realized how right she was.

Preston insisted on driving me home, so I let him take me downtown. Close to the tower, but not close enough for him to know my final destination. I couldn't let him take me all the way. He'd never understand. He didn't want to let me go when I insisted on getting out of the car.

"I don't like the idea of just dropping you off, Lily. I'm not that kind of man. I take care of what's mine."

*His?* My head spun with dizziness, my emotions out of control. I wanted to be Preston's more than anything, but I was already Dorian's. I even had the fucking brand to prove it. I shook my head. "I'm sorry. I really do need to go."

He lifted the strands of my hair from my neck, exposing the tattoo as he stared at it. "I'm not stupid, Lily. I know you are deliberately avoiding telling me things about you. You won't even give me the courtesy of telling me where you live. But you have to believe there is not a fucking thing in the goddamn world that you could tell me that would make me not want you."

I wanted to tell him. I wanted to believe him, but I'd lived too long in this current state, and I knew exactly what Dorian could do. He was not someone to trifle with. I had already taken a great risk by going to Preston's and staying so late. I had a bad feeling about what lay ahead for me when I walked in that door. I pressed my lips to Preston's, and he kissed me. His hand tangled in my hair, then he pulled back. Fisting my hair in his hand, he tugged my head back so that my gaze found his. "Don't go."

My eyes closed then fluttered open. "I have to. Please. You have to trust me."

"How can I trust you when you won't give me anything to trust?"

"Trust that . . ." Dare I say it? What harm would it do? He might think it too sudden, but we'd been dancing around this relationship for a few months now. We were close friends, and now, lovers. And besides, I'd probably never get another chance to tell him if I didn't take it now. "Trust that I love you, Preston," I said, then opened the door and quickly got out of the car. I glanced around at the empty sidewalk and then disappeared from Preston's sight before he could even open his car door to stop me.

# CHAPTER 11

Preston

"Lily!" I shouted at the closed window as she de-materialized from my sight.

"Fuck!

"Fuck!

"Fuck!"

I banged my hands on the steering wheel. She was a puzzle with many facets. Her elusiveness frustrated the hell out of me, and her iron will would surely be the death of me. I didn't know if I admired that about her or hated it. But I'd known from the start that she was stubborn. From the beginning, she'd presented herself as someone who knew how to take care of herself. She'd been on this earth a long time. Had been a vampire long enough to know how to survive. Most likely seen things most women hadn't. She was tough; there was no doubt about that. But I worried.

I worried because she'd told me she loved me.

Not that I didn't want that. I'd even thought about loving her, but I sensed her declaration was given out of desperation and fear that she might never be with me again.

I trolled the streets for another hour, looking for her dark purple coat, though deep down I knew I wouldn't find her. I had to give up as the first light of day peeked over the bay bridge. I was about to get caught out in the sun, and I was still twenty minutes from the mansion. My eyes stung from the glare, and I slipped my glasses down over them so I could see the road. When I turned the corner, all cars ahead stood at a standstill. I'd hit the morning commute traffic. The twenty-minute drive to the mansion would now take me forty-five. Even if I tried to dematerialize back home, I'd lose too much energy and tumble to the ground. I wasn't even sure I could. I considered just getting out of the car and trying to walk to shelter, but I feared someone would see me, think I needed help, and take me to the local hospital. I'd never survive that. My energy level had plummeted so fast, it was already almost completely gone.

I was fucked.

When traffic cleared, and I had a chance to move again, my car wouldn't go. The engine had died. I tried to start it, but it wouldn't even turn over. Fuck. Now what? I glanced at the gas gauge and realized it was on empty. I'd been so focused on finding Lily, I hadn't bothered to check the gas level.

I sat inside the car, trying to make myself disappear without success when someone knocked on the window.

"Hey, dude. Move your car!"

*Jesus. Now what am I supposed to do?*

He pounded against the glass again. "Hey, asshole! Can you fucking hear me? Move your goddamn car! I need to get to work!"

I wished I could. When I didn't respond, he cursed something unintelligible and strutted away. I had to try something. I managed to crawl into the back seat and crouched down on the floor. Luckily, this was a large Lincoln sedan, and the back seat was more than adequate for a vampire.

At that moment, I squeezed my eyes shut and concentrated with everything I had. A few seconds later, I found myself on the sidewalk with the sun glaring down on me. I hadn't gotten very far when my energy gave out. My chest hurt, my limbs ached, the joints swollen with Rheumatoid arthritis—one of the first symptoms of sun damage for a vampire.

My eyesight blurred as I looked around. People ignored me as I huddled on the sidewalk close to the wall, most likely thinking I was a homeless vagrant strung out on drugs, particularly since I was shirtless and shoeless.

I spotted an alleyway. It wouldn't shield me completely, but maybe there was a dumpster I could climb into. Pulling myself forward on my arms and stomach, I crawled toward the alley and turned the corner. The shade was only on one side, and I stayed in it. It didn't stop the degeneration of my cells, but it slowed the process enough for me to see down the small street. "Fuck." There were only two small trashcans set out. Nothing that my body would fit into. I inched my way to them and positioned myself between the two cans and the brick wall. My body shook with chills and burned with fever as I huddled there, unable to move. There was nothing else I could do. I didn't think the sun would kill me, but the damage it was doing to my blood cells would take several days for me to recover from. That was if the damage didn't get any worse. But the longer I stayed out, the worse it would get.

When Lily had said she loved me, perhaps she was psychic and realized she might never see me again. That this was my end. I wished I'd told her the same. It was stupid of me to stay out so long looking for her. But I'd only had Lily on my mind. I hadn't given a fucking thought to what might happen to me.

I didn't recall ever hearing of a vampire who'd died from sun exposure, but then again, I'd never heard anything about what happened to someone left in the sun for longer than a few minutes. Most vamps were smart enough not to get themselves into this kind of predicament.

My chest hurt, and my breathing had become labored and was getting more difficult by the minute. My mouth was so dry, my tongue stuck to the roof of my mouth, and I could literally feel my insides drying out, shriveling up like a piece of fruit inside a dehydration machine that someone had turned on high.

My mind traveled to a vision of Lily under me. She'd been everything I'd dreamed about for the past few months and more. I couldn't have asked for a sweeter time. Then the vision disappeared. I couldn't concentrate on her anymore. Was my brain shriveling up along with the rest of my insides? I held up my hand close to my eyes. The tips of my fingers were shriveled. My skin was scaly, and some of it flaked off the back of my hand.

Unable to hold up my head any longer, I lowered it to the ground, my eyelids too heavy to remain open. No longer conscious of what or who I was, I drifted into darkness.

# CHAPTER 12

Lily

*I* couldn't have asked for a more wonderful first experience of real lovemaking. Preston and I had had such a beautiful encounter. I had loved lying with him on that giant bed of his. The things he'd done to please me brought shivers to my body even now. The story of his turning had enthralled me. Not only was he great in bed, but he was a wonderful storyteller.

As I vanished from Preston's sight, all I could think was how much I hated leaving him sitting in the car, shouting my name. That was the last thought I had of Preston because the moment I materialized inside my room, all those lovely moments were a thing of the past. Never to be spoken of or thought about again.

Dorian sat on the red velvet lounge in my room, waiting for me as I materialized.

"Hello, love."

"Dorian." My hand went to my heart. "You . . . startled me." He was here, home from his trip early—*two days* early.

"Meant to. Where've you been?" His tone was casual, too calm for him to be sitting there so still, waiting for me—which I had no doubt he'd been doing. He lifted the small tumbler he held to his lips and took a small sip of the brown liquid, then lowered his arm, resting the glass on the armrest. The silk pajama pants he wore suggested he'd been home for a while. That meant he knew that I'd been gone for most of the night. Shit. I hadn't counted on him coming home so soon. I had to think fast about where I'd been, but there was only one excuse I could give him that he would accept.

"Nowhere special. Just dealing the last of your heroin." I shrugged out of my coat and went to my closet to hang it up.

He sighed, then placed the glass down on the small table beside the lounge and stood. As he walked toward me, his brown eyes turned darker. "Lily, I know there wasn't any more shit to sell."

"No. There was. Malik must have held some back because he had some left. He gave me a few more bags to sell so I could make up the cash I lost the other night."

"You think I'm stupid?"

"Of course not."

"Then why do you feed me lies that I know couldn't possibly be true?"

"I'm not lying."

"Okay, then where's the cash?"

"I already gave it to Malik," I lied and prayed Malik would back me up.

Before I knew or even saw him move, Dorian stood in front of me. He pressed me up against the wall, his hand squeezing my throat, his eyes dark with rage, and his face contorted to kill. I struggled to breathe as I stared back at him, my fingers clawing at his hands to release me. "I should kill you now, get it over with. The prospect of ending you has been something I've been contemplating. Or should I kill Julian?" he said through gritted teeth, his fangs glistening. My panic intensified at his words. "If I didn't have a fondness for your brother, I would kill you both. Be done with you. I'm getting bored with the responsibility, to tell you the truth."

He released his grip from around my neck and turned from me. I coughed, my hands massaging my throat.

Then he whirled back at me, pressing me up against the wall again, but he didn't choke me this time, just pinned me. He was much stronger than I was. He always would be. Dorian had made me, giving me his blood. I only had a portion of the strength he had. He could kill me so easily, but in all these years, he never had. But he didn't love me. He tolerated me. Kept me under his so-called protection. Kept other vampires from having me. Though he'd never wanted me for himself, he made it clear that no other male could touch me. Was that his way of torturing me? Depriving me of the pleasure I'd only just discovered with Preston? Dorian didn't love me. He loved Julian. But Julian would only perform when he was weak, forced to wear silver, or lately, drugged with that Blaze drug Dorian had found that worked on vampires. Unable to defend himself. Dorian kept me so Julian would do his bidding. Julian protected me, and I protected Julian.

"Dorian, please," I begged. "I'll do better. I'm sorry. I won't ever lie to you again. I promise."

"What happened to you, Lily? Where did that timid little girl I'd grown to admire disappear to? You know the one. The scared little girl who begged me not to hurt her and her brother. The virgin I've been protecting for the past century. Tell me, Lily, where did she go?"

He bit his lower lip and tilted his head and grinned. "You are still a virgin, are you not?"

I nodded, trying my best to hide the lie I'd just promised never to tell again.

"Ah, Lily, you make me do such hurtful things. Things I don't want to do. Hurting you is never my intention, but I need you to obey me. Now, tell me, where were you all night?"

"I told you. I was out selling for you. It was hard to find buyers. I had to visit almost all of my clients. That's a lot of territory to cover in one night. But no one was buying. I finally found a couple of junkies down in the Marina district who were just coming down from a high. I'm sorry I was so late. I went straight to Malik, knowing he would be worried. I gave him the money. I swear."

I watched Dorian's Adam's apple move as he swallowed. He nodded. "Okay. I believe you," he said and then stepped away from me.

The tension weighing down my shoulders refused to ease even though Dorian seemed to believe me. The possibility of him suddenly turning back around and punishing me anyway was always very high. Dorian's moods changed faster than I could track. He could be as gentle as a kitten at times, then as mean and sly as a viper the next moment.

He headed for the door but turned back before leaving. "Next time, don't expect me to be so forgiving." Then he left. I sighed, shrouded with both sadness and relief at the sound of the door locking. Frustration grew within me because I knew the moment the lock turned, the walls became impenetrable, as well. I was Dorian's prisoner again. Both Julian and I were. Death was surely better than this.

I went to my bed, taking my pillow in my arms, caressing it as if it could comfort me when I all I really wanted was to know that Preston would forgive me for leaving the way I had and that my brother was okay.

I thought about Preston and how easy it had been to talk to him. Recounting the experience of how we had become what we were. It had been so many years since I'd thought about it, I'd had to stop the story. I had trouble remembering exactly the way it had all happened.

*WE'D BEEN RUNNING for what seemed like hours, dodging horses and carriages, ducking into alleyways, and hiding in alcoves and behind anything we happened upon. Our neighbor, Mrs. Rosen, was dead. Blood pooled around her head, her neck had been torn to shreds by some sick creature. We were scared that whatever had done that to her, was still inside, so we ran. After hours of running and hiding, our clothes were covered with mud from the rain-soaked roads we'd been trekking through. The air was cold and wet. And help was nowhere in sight. The sky was so dark, and clouds shrouded the stars and poured rain down so fast it blurred our vision. There was no place to hide. We were cold, hungry, and drenched to the bone when Julian suggested we go home. He was convinced that whatever monster had murdered Mrs. Rosen would be long gone and that the police would have come and discovered her body. The monster would have fled. I agreed, so we headed home. Though the minute we entered our apartment, we instantly realized we'd been wrong.*

*Julian towered over me as the dark figure stood in front of us in the small living space we called home. Except for the trickle of moonlight coming in from the window, the room was mostly dark, and all I could make out was the black-hooded cloak and the pale hand that gripped my brother's neck, snatching him up as if he were no heavier than a ragdoll. Julian's body seemed lifeless, his mind not registering what was happening to him. I wanted him to struggle and fight.*

*I wanted to scream, but the creature's eyes glowed with a golden hue as they locked with mine, and my body froze as the scream that had been on my lips became nothing more than silent air. My limbs were paralyzed, unable to move. The monster threw back the hood of his cloak and continued to hold my gaze with his. Time froze, and the air in the room stilled as I continued to stare at his face. A beautiful face. So handsome.*

*The vampire dragged his golden orbs from mine and gazed upon my brother's face with a reverence I'd never seen anyone possess before. He held Julian's flaccid body close to him, kissed my brother's cheek, and then slowly, with care, sank his fangs into Julian's neck. Not viciously. But with great care.*

I SWIPED AWAY the tears that soaked my cheeks. Was that the way it had happened? I couldn't recall exactly . . .

Why had Julian and I been given this fate? If we had stayed on the farm after our parents died, we never would have been in Dorian's path. We never would have been turned into vampires. Now it was all just wishes and regret for something that could never change.

# CHAPTER 13

Preston

*D*arkness caressed me, shrouding me in a blanket of nothing. I had no thoughts, no desires, no needs; just blankness and the sensation of floating through weightless space. I was positive that death had come for me, and I was disappointed. Where was the heaven or the hell I'd been told about? There was no great light of sanctuary or fire of torture. Just . . . nothing. A world devoid of everything.

As time slipped away, streaks of red and orange filtered in, gravity became my enemy, and I knew that death had eluded me. The heaviness turned into pain and grew to a point where I wanted to die. My eyes fluttered open to blurred faces. I quickly closed them, wanting to return to the calm of nothing. Why the fuck did every bone and muscle in my body ache and burn?

"Hey, he's waking up!" I heard Gage say, his voice too close to my face for my comfort.

"Step aside. Let me examine him." Another male voice: Grayson,

Chelle's dad; now, our vampire doctor. Cold fingers touched my face. One dipping the bottom of my eye down as bright light glared into it. Something cold pressed down on my chest. I opened my eyes to see him hovering over me, listening to whatever he heard through that stethoscope of his. He was a new vampire—new this century, I mean —turned in his early thirties if I had to guess. Chelle had been five at the time and had witnessed her mother's death. He was a good doctor, but I didn't want him prodding and probing me with his hands or his instruments. My skin hurt at every touch.

"Stop." My voice was low, barely audible to even my own ears.

"Is he going to be okay?" Cian's voice of concern asked. He was the rock behind the Lost Boys. The level-headed one of the twinsey pack. He was grounded and strong-minded. He had a great sense for business and kept us together . . . kept us a family. He was the center of everything that made us whole. His woman, Maggie, looked petite and angelic as she stood by his side.

"He should be. I've never seen anyone who's been out in daylight as long as he was. It will take a few days for his insides to return to normal again. The cells need to replenish. You're lucky Ari and Vanessa were able to locate you. If you'd have stayed outside much longer, I'm not sure how long it would take for your organs to hydrate again. *If* they would."

"Elvis, buddy, you scared the piss out of me," Gage's face hovered over me again. His long, unruly curls flowed over his cheeks as he looked down. He smiled and nodded. "Glad you're back among the living."

I glanced around. Most of the faces were still blurred to my eyes, but I suspected that the entire household stood in my room.

"How . . .?" I asked.

"I have your blood in me. Remember? You guys thought it would be a good idea if all of you gave me some. Just for this very reason. Bet you never considered the possibility of a human saving your ass." Ari beamed, priding himself on his human ability to walk in the sunlight.

"If I didn't have your blood," Ari continued, "I never would have known you were missing."

"Luckily, V can walk in the sun," Lane added with a grin. Cocky son of a bitch. "She teleported Ari to you in that alley." I glanced at the witch-turned-vampire. Damn. I never would have thought I'd be thankful that Lane had turned the witch. Guess she wasn't so bad, after all.

"Here," Grayson stuck a straw attached to a plastic bag of blood into my mouth. "You need more nourishment. I've already given you two bags intravenously, but the more you ingest, the better."

I swallowed; the sensation almost foreign to me. I hadn't realized my throat was so dry.

"What the hell were you doing out there?" Gage asked.

"Searching." That came out like a whisper. As hard as I tried to talk louder, the volume of the words wouldn't increase.

"Searching for what or whom?" Cian asked.

"Lily. She . . ." I shook my head. These guys were never going to understand. "She left me sitting in the car. Wouldn't let me take her all the way home. How long have I been out?"

"Four days," Grayson answered.

"Four days? I need to get up. I need to find her." I tried to move, but my body wasn't having any of it.

"Rest for now."

"Where does she live?" Lane asked. "You never did say." He had his arm around Vanessa. She was hot for a witch. I'd always thought so, but more so now that she'd helped save my life. She looked tough standing there with her hands on her hips and her don't-fuck-with-me attitude. She and Lane were good together. Ever since she'd come into his life, he seemed to be a bit less of a jerk, particularly when V was around. Her brazen demeanor made me ache for Lily.

"Maybe she lives in a run-down neighborhood and didn't want you to see her house," Chelle said, and everyone looked at her as if she'd just grown three tits. She shrugged. "Just sayin'. After being here and seeing how we live, maybe she was embarrassed."

"Vampires don't live in run-down neighborhoods or houses. They don't want for anything. The world is theirs for the taking," Lane said. "Usually," he added when Vanessa frowned at him.

"She's definitely hiding something from me."

"She probably just doesn't want to see your ugly ass anymore," Gage scoffed. "Don't be so stupid next time, son. Come home before curfew; that way you won't get caught out without shoes and a shirt in the fucking sunlight." He walked out of the room then. Gage was my best friend, but he had shit for tact when it came to voicing his emotions. I smiled. Nice to have someone worry about me.

IT TOOK me over a week to recuperate completely. There were several times I'd considered risking it and continuing my search for Lily, but I really had no clue where to start except the bar. I could sit there and wait and hope that she'd show up. However, every time I tried to get dressed, my breath became labored, my body ached, and I was unable to teleport anywhere. Driving wasn't an option since my vision hadn't cleared all the way either.

It had been rather amusing watching Gage attend to me, though. At his insistence. His doting brought back memories from my past. Ones I had only recently spoken about.

I needed a shower. I'd taken a couple during my convalescence but always felt so weak afterwards. My sunstroke—as everyone had come to refer to my sickness—must have been similar to a bad strain of one of the many human flu viruses combined with pneumonia.

When I stepped out of the shower and walked into my room, I spotted Gage sitting on the window seat sofa, gazing out into the night. He wore jeans with a Guns 'n' Roses T-shirt, and his long, curly, golden locks were pulled back into a ponytail. The scent of his Creed cologne permeated the air of my room, coating it with hints of citrus and jasmine.

An opened bottle of Johnny Walker's premium blue label blend sat on the shelf of the credenza with an empty glass next to it. Looked like my man had some great expectations for the evening, bringing out the good stuff at no less than a hundred and fifty dollars a bottle.

I held the towel around my waist and headed to my closet, grabbed a pair of jeans, and slipped them on. After I had finished dressing, I headed to the credenza and poured myself a glass of the very fine scotch, bringing it with me to stand just behind Gage. The bridge was alight with headlights heading into the city on one side, and red brake lights on the other as cars took off toward Sausalito, another tourist trap just north of San Francisco.

"I thought I'd lost you." The gravelly quality of Gage's voice tore me to shreds.

"Don't," I barked, not wanting to get all sentimental.

"Why the fuck not? We've been friends for centuries. Pretty damn close, too, if you ask me. Am I not supposed to have any feelings? How would you feel if it had been me?"

I sucked in my lips. He was right. I'd have cared. Probably would have cared too much. I walked around the sofa and sat a few feet away, facing the window. "It would wreck me," I said, and feeling the heaviness of that emotion build up in my throat, I added, "But how about if we not dwell on the morbidity of that. I made a fucking mistake, but I'm fine." He glanced in my direction. I made a silly face at him. He hit me on the back of the head with the palm of his hand. "Ouch, Dad. Stop it."

Gage took a sip of his whiskey and returned his gaze to the window. "I'll help you look for her."

I glanced at him. "Thank you."

He nodded. "We'll find her. No leaf unturned."

I inhaled and chuckled. "That's stone."

"What?"

"No stone unturned."

"Stone, leaf, who the fuck cares? Means the same thing."

Normally, I'd have argued that the ridiculous saying declared the efforts taken during a search and tell him that the stone was heavier and therefore harder to turn, making the task more difficult, but what was the point? This was Gage. Plus, I didn't have the energy. Love sucked.

"It's Friday. Let's go check out one of those parties at Sweet's Delicacies tonight."

"What happened to looking for Lily?" I asked.

Gage shrugged. "No leaf unturned. Maybe somebody there will know her."

"I doubt that." What would my Lily be doing at a party where all the guests were either whores or paying for whores?

"You never know. I'm sure there will be a lot of vampires there. Someone might know something about her. It's worth a try."

"I guess."

"Gage has a point," Cian said as he entered my room, wearing a pair of dark gray slacks that hung low on his waist and a long-sleeve, purple-and-white-striped button-down. He looked ready for a night of partying. "If she lives somewhere in the city, someone at the party might know where."

Lane stood in the door jamb; his long, dark hair flowing loosely over his arms and stopping just at his elbows. He was dressed equally as well but with black slacks and a light pink shirt. "Can't go to the party with you guys, though." Lane sounded truly disappointed, and I bet he was.

"We promised Magdalena and Vanessa we'd take them out tonight," Cian said.

Lane shrugged. "Something about double dating and how fun it would be. Anyway, it's too late to back out of that now." Lane's eyebrows briefly knitted together, and he rubbed his thumb and forefinger over them. "If you've ever seen V when she's upset or mad, I'm sure you'll understand why."

"Yeah." I nodded in understanding. V could be a wicked witch and had unfathomable powers. She was not to be messed with. I understood completely, and smiled a little to myself, appreciating her ability to bring a wiseass like Lane to his knees.

# CHAPTER 14

Lily

No one had come into my room since Dorian left; the passing of days registered only by the rise and fall of the blinds. If I'd kept count correctly, it was six, maybe even seven days—a week of loneliness where I'd been locked away in this prison. I prayed each night when dawn rolled around that the blinds would close on schedule and Dorian hadn't tampered with them.

Malik hadn't even come in to give me any blood, and I grew tired and weak from the lack of nourishment. Today, I hadn't even bothered to get out of bed. Maybe Dorian had left me here to rot.

I had no form of entertainment either. No phone, computer, flat screen, or even a book to read. Well, I did have one book. One I'd kept with me, hidden from Dorian. The pages were frail from my having read it so many times, and at this point I was afraid to even open Anne Rice's *Interview with a Vampire* for fear that the pages would fall out. It was a fictional book, of course, but one that aligned so closely to our own lives that I could have sworn she'd been writing about us. It was a book gifted to me by an acquaintance of Dorian's and Julian's, Langdon Atwell, who'd taken an interest in both my and Julian's relationship with his friend. I held the book in my hands, clutching it to my chest as I lay back on my bed. I didn't need to read it. I'd memorized every word a long time ago. Just holding it close to me was a comfort. My eyes, heavy from lack of blood and boredom, closed as the story of that day repeated in my head.

*I'D BEEN SITTING by the wall reading a new book, a gift from Langdon, as the men played poker at a table a few feet away from me. I had wanted to play, but the book had managed to captivate me and kept me completely enthralled until the sounds from the table drew me in, and I glanced up. Langdon glanced in my direction. I lowered my gaze back to the book in my lap to avoid his stare. His glances were happening too often over the course of the game, and I feared Dorian might misinterpret the man's concerns for my well-being as affection. Maybe it was affection. But I never gave him reason to show me any kindness. Yet, still, he'd insisted that I take the book he'd given to me. He claimed it was a gift to help me get through the many lonely nights he knew I faced. At the time, I wasn't sure how he knew I spent most of my time alone. I'd thanked him and taken the book. I began reading it immediately, and couldn't bring myself to put it down until I finished it, which so happened, wasn't until days later—when I was able to bring myself to pick it back up again after that night.*

*My brother sat on Dorian's right. Langdon next to Julian. It was a small game, only the three of them left as the fourth had excused himself hours before, having lost all his money earlier in the evening.*

*From the position of my seat against the wall, I noticed Langdon and Julian playing footsies under the table. I'd suspected something was going on between the two, but this action confirmed my suspicions.*

*To make matters worse, Langdon placed his hand in Julian's lap and then said, "Dorian, you must let me take Lily to live with me."*

*I froze in my seat. Why was he asking this? His hand was in my brother's lap, yet he was asking for me?*

*Both Dorian's and Julian's gaze instantly darted to Langdon. Julian* smiled—a sweet brotherly smile as he glanced in my direction with hope in his eyes. Dorian scowled and picked up the tumbler full of whiskey laced with blood beside him and sipped.

"I need her here," Dorian retorted and looked back down at his cards. The scowl was still prominent on his forehead, and I wondered if he suspected anything about what was going on under the table with Julian and Langdon. Maybe Langdon's request was just a ruse to throw Dorian off about his affection for Julian. I suddenly feared for my brother.

Julian stayed quiet. He knew better than to interfere, though I guessed he was secretly pleased to have someone take an interest in my well-being, even if it was Langdon, whom he was also fond of. Even though he was messing around with Langdon, Julian had seemed content—or at least accepting of his fate—living with Dorian, our maker. But like me, I knew he longed for something more or different.

"Really, Dorian," Langdon went on. "What do you need her for? You have Julian. He's your lover. Let Lily come to stay with me. I can make her happy. Let the woman go. You never pay any attention to her. You simply keep her at your beck and call, only so you can keep Julian in line and have someone to take out in public to hide your true sexual orientation. Lily needs a real man. Someone who can give her orgasms."

He'd gone too far challenging Dorian's manhood, and I trembled with dread as I glanced at my brother, who'd stayed compliant.

"You play with Julian under the table, and you think I don't see." My brother's eyes shot to Dorian's, fear evident in them. "And then you have the balls to ask for Lily?"

An enormous amount of fear enveloped me as Dorian rose from his seat, and in a flick of an eye, grabbed Langdon around the neck, shoving him back against the wall right next to where I sat. I jumped up, moving away. A sword, a beautiful memento of Dorian's time in the Revolutionary War, embellished with carvings along with Dorian's initials hung above their heads. As Doran's grip around Langdon's neck tightened, his free hand reached up and took that mighty saber in his hands . . .

.   .   .

MY SCREAMS JOLTED ME AWAKE, and I sat up on my bed, panting with horror.

My hands massaged my neck, even though it hadn't been my head that had been severed. But the vision of Langdon's head rolling across the carpet still haunted me, the fear of knowing how ruthless Dorian really was fresh in my mind. Dorian had killed Langdon that night in a jealous rage. Though he'd claimed it was the poker game that had gone south. "Tainted with bad blood," he'd said. He was right about that part. Both Julian and I knew the truth, but we never spoke of it.

My brother, who, at the time had been one of Dorian's best friends, stayed by his side whenever they were in mixed company. I, on the other hand, was known as Dorian's wife, and accompanied him to all of his social functions. I was for show, something to be paraded around like a show dog since the gay subculture of San Francisco hadn't gained any viable visibility until the early nineteen eighties. Homophobia ran rampant, and the acceptance of homosexuality had been non-existent at the time. Gays were highly stigmatized as unnatural. That sort of lifestyle would have put a blockade in the path of Dorian's rise to fame and fortune, and his acceptance as an honorable and respected businessman.

It wasn't until recently that Julian had decided he'd had enough of Dorian and rebelled against him. The times had changed, and Dorian really didn't need me anymore. Julian wanted to leave and discover other possibilities, and of course, he couldn't leave without me. He was tired of living a life as a secret lover. Giving Dorian—our maker and one who'd never been able to accept rejection—two options: kill us or imprison us. At the time, he hadn't had the heart to kill Julian. And I believe he actually loved my brother. I think he only kept me so that Julian would do his bidding, hanging the balance of my life over my brother's head. That and the Blaze, which kept Julian from fighting back. I suspected Dorian used the Blaze on Julian frequently, though he'd never injected me with it.

There was a time—one of those rare moments when Julian and I were sequestered away together without Dorian or someone else's supervision—when Julian had confessed to me that he enjoyed being with the females who paid for his services as much as he did the males. Though, of course, he'd like nothing better than to escape and live his life the way he chose. We'd made plans, several times over the years, but they'd never panned out for some reason or another. The threat of the sword at our necks usually at the forefront of our minds.

The sound of the lock turning in the door startled me. I quickly shoved the book I'd been caressing under my pillow.

I was relieved to see Malik. He held a bag of blood in his left hand and toted a young human male by the arm with the other, depositing him on the floor in front of me. The human sank to his knees and lowered his gaze, obviously under Malik's compulsion. He was skinny and didn't look much older than Julian. He stayed on his knees and tilted his head to the side. His artery throbbed, pounding so hard, the beat reverberated in my head, calling to me. On instinct, I licked my lips in anticipation.

"Drink this first." Malik shoved the plastic bag at me. "Then take from him. Don't want you killing him because you're starving. Boss wants you to be strong for this evening. He's having a small get-together."

It was Friday. I'd been lucky enough to have missed last week's party. The human's fresh blood would give me more energy, and ingesting from the bag first was a good idea. I had no desire to hurt the boy, and as hungry as I was, there was no telling if I'd be able to stop once I started. After I finished the bag, I took the boy's arm and sank my fangs into his wrist. He looked up at me, his eyes blank the entire time I sucked at his vein. As I drank, all I could think of was how young he was, and how sorry I felt for him to be in this situation. I wasn't ashamed of taking his blood. I'd taken blood from plenty of humans over the years, compelling them to succumb to my will and offer me their vein. But this time? I'd never do this to someone. This time, the young man was Dorian's slave. No longer able to come and go as he pleased. Completely under the control of vampires every day until he was sold to the highest bidder.

When I finished nourishing myself, I looked up to find Malik rummaging through my closet.

"What are you doing?"

"I'm looking for the light green gown Dorian bought you. He wants you to wear that tonight. Ah. Here it is."

He pulled the gown out of the closet and placed it on my bed. The gown screamed *promiscuity*, and I'd never worn it. It was too revealing, and every male in the room would no doubt stare at me. I could already feel the way their eyes would drag up and down my body. The low-cut silk bodice trimmed with lace exposed half my bosom as the opening dipped down almost to my belly button. One wrong move and my breasts would pop right out, exposing them completely. Besides that, only the lacy part covered the nipple and had no lining, making it very see-through.

"Why does Dorian want me to wear that dress?" I'd never really been sure why he purchased it. He'd never asked me to wear it before. He never wanted to see that much of my skin. The back of the dress dipped down even farther than the front, stopping right at the top of the crack of my ass. And the skirt matched the lace at the top—again no lining to speak of other than a thin strip of silk down the center and the back. It would take a lot of double-sided tape and a miracle to keep the dress from slipping. It was tight at the hips, too, which tugged when I walked, pulling at the top. I'd hated it when it was given to me and had stuck it way in the back of my closet behind several coats, hoping that Dorian would forget about it.

"I believe he wants to show you off to the guests."

"Show me off? For what purpose? I thought I was supposed to be his wife. What about his reputation? A decent and caring husband would never want his wife parading around in that . . . that . . . monstrosity."

Then, the light bulb went off in my head as I stared at Malik, who seemed reluctant to talk to me. The sadness in his eyes told me all I needed to know. Dorian wanted to sell me. Or, at least sell my services. He'd never asked me to do that before, knowing I was a virgin. Correction, *had been* a virgin, but he didn't know things had changed. He couldn't possibly know that. Could he? He'd claimed on more than one occasion that he'd been saving me for something, though I'd never asked him to elaborate on that, never wanting to be saved for anything or anyone. I guess tonight was that night.

"I'm sorry, Lily," Malik said in a low, soft voice as he walked away, snatching the human's arm as they headed for the door. Then he stopped and turned his head toward me. "If it's any consolation, I did try to talk him out of it, but one can only try to persuade Dorian to a certain degree without fear of upsetting him."

I nodded. My hands shook as I swiped away the tears that dripped down my cheeks.

"You have thirty minutes to shower and get dressed. Please don't dawdle. I don't think I can take watching what might happen if you're not upstairs when he's ready."

# CHAPTER 15

Preston

Sweet Towers was located in the heart of the city, smack dab downtown, just south of the Market district. The forty-nine-story building was the second tallest building in San Francisco. Everything above the fifth floor was strictly for residential use. The top of the tower was curved to resemble a translucent crystal.

"Wow, this place is something, huh?" Gage said as we stood on the sidewalk and looked up. "There are forty-nine floors, but the top floor is listed as number fifty."

I glanced at him in question, and he continued. "No thirteenth floor. Superstitions."

"Ahhh." I nodded, looking up at the bluish-gray-tinted windows. "Does this building have the one-way glass?"

"Nah. Not too many buildings around the city do. I'm guessing the cost might be a factor."

"Or maybe our illustrious Mr. Sweet just doesn't know about it."

"You're probably right since this is the priciest place to live on the West Coast."

"Parking must be a bitch," I said as we headed in through the double glass doors.

"I think they have a subterranean garage located several floors under the building."

As we entered the building, I was immediately awestruck by the originality of the décor. A large statue—maybe about twelve feet high—of what was clearly a male vampire pressing his opened mouth to the vein of a woman's neck sat in the middle of the lobby. The male's hand disappeared under the female's long, flowing dress as she lay draped across his other arm. Her eyes were closed, her breasts exposed. Her expression was one of complete and utter ecstasy.

"Wow!" Gage said and cupped himself. I was certain he was entertaining the prospect of reenacting that very same pose soon. "I can't wait to meet this guy."

"It's a little *in your face* if you ask me," I said, having eyes only for Lily. "Interesting that he's not the least bit concerned about humans' beliefs about vampirism."

Gage shrugged. "There's all sorts of art about vampires floating around the city."

"True." I nodded.

"Don't think too hard on it, Elvis." He patted me on the back. "There's blood to drink and women to fuck." I rolled my eyes, not having the slightest desire to fuck anyone but Lily.

"And make inquires about Lily," I added.

"Right. Come on." Gage pointed to two heavy doors. "There's the elevator." Above it read: *Express to Sky Deck* in big bold letters.

We stepped in, and Gage hit the single round button labeled *Sky Deck* engraved in gold tone, set inside an intricate gold oval metal design. It was a long ride up, even though the elevator seemed to whiz by all the other floors at an excessive speed. When we stepped out, a familiar vampire wearing a black suit, gold tie, and a lighter shade of gold shirt greeted us.

"Jace, my man," Gage said. "You remember us. From the poker game?"

He nodded. "Follow me. Malik is inside."

"Malik?" I questioned the unfamiliar name as my feet sank into plush, gold carpeting. Gold carpet? The hallway walls were painted a deep, rich red. A striking contrast to the floor.

Jace turned toward me. "Malik Roach. The vampire you beat in the poker game."

"Right, Malik." Stetson hat, Roach guy. What a name.

"You'll be pleased to know that Mr. Sweet himself will be here tonight," Jace informed us as he led us through a set of double wooden doors.

"He doesn't attend all his parties?"

"No. He is a very busy man and can only make it for a select few. These parties are very private and held with the utmost discretion. Guests are here by invitation only and carefully selected. Mr. Sweet has a reputation to uphold around the city, and if things were to . . . leak out about what happens at these parties, well, I don't think he'd appreciate that much. So, what you see here, stays here. Otherwise . . ." He swiped his forefinger across his throat and smiled. "Understand?"

"Yeah. We get it," I said. Normally, something like that would have set off an alarm in my head, but these were vampires after all, and most vampires marched to a different beat than humans.

"Good."

"We must be the select," Gage whispered, and Jace smirked, clearly able to hear him. "We are about to meet the illustrious Mr. Sweet himself." Gage's eyebrows waggled up and down. I truly wasn't as impressed as Gage.

About twenty-five people—or vampires, it was hard to tell—stood around talking. It looked like an ordinary but casual cocktail party.

"So posh," Gage whispered.

"Too posh, if you ask me."

As we stepped farther into the room, we were both handed a small cordial glass of something green. I sniffed. "Absinthe?"

Gage made a what-the-hell face and downed the entire drink. Shit.

I turned to ask Jace which one of the vampires was Sweet, but he'd disappeared.

"I guess we're on our own now," I said to Gage, and he smiled and took another glass from the platter of a passing waiter.

"Gentlemen," a deep voice greeted from our right, and I turned to see that Roach guy from the poker game, sans Stetson hat. He wore comfortable-looking silk lounge pants with his shirt open, hanging loosely. I suddenly felt way overdressed in my torn jeans and black T-shirt. I imagined how out of place Jace must feel in the suit he wore. As I glanced around, I noticed that some of the males were shirtless, and the women were almost naked except for sexy underwear or other revealing garments.

"Glad you could make it. Missed you two at the poker game last week. I'd really like a chance to win back some of my money. Hope you show up next week. I don't think we were ever formally intro-duced. Name's Malik Roach." He held out his large, dark hand to me, and I took it so we could shake.

"Preston."

Then he shook Gage's hand. "I'm Gage. Thanks for the invite. It looks like the party's been going on for a while."

Malik looked around and grinned, white teeth gleaming against his dark complexion. "Yes, for about an hour or so now. I'd like to introduce you to your host. Dorian, I'd like you to meet our newest guests." The man standing just on the other side of Malik with his back to us turned to face us.

I dropped my glass. Green, sticky liquid pooled on the gold carpet by my feet. No one seemed to care.

"Preston? My word, Preston!" Dorian smiled and wrapped his arms around my shoulders, hugging me to him. The embrace seemed to go on and on.

He pushed back and eyed my face. "Is it really you?"

I swallowed and nodded the best I could. Dorian was the last vampire on earth I'd thought to see here in San Francisco, especially owning several buildings and hosting sex parties.

"Yes," I cleared the lump in my throat.

"You know him?" Gage asked.

Then Dorian kissed me on the mouth, his lips moving over mine with affection. I didn't return the kiss, but I didn't shove him away either. I couldn't. I was too shocked. His fang scraped against my lower lip, drawing blood, and then his tongue swept over it, sealing the tiny wound.

"I guess you do," Gage added with a chuckle. When Dorian stopped kissing me, I rubbed my finger over my bottom lip where the sting of Dorian's nip lingered.

"I apologize," he said, and licked his lips.

"What are you doing here?"

"Well, this is my party."

"Yeah. I get that. But . . . I thought you were . . ." I hesitated, not sure how to approach the situation.

He smiled. "Forgive me. Of course you wouldn't know. I own this building as well as a few other properties here in the city."

Gage cleared his throat beside me, reminding me that he was there. Fuck. I wasn't looking forward to the unavoidable conversation I knew would happen later.

"Dorian, this is my friend, Gage."

"Gage. My, you're a big one. Are there more at home like you?" Dorian laughed and waved his hand as if sending that thought away. "Well, any friend of Preston's is a friend of mine. Welcome. Please, make yourselves at home and enjoy. We have an assortment of sweet delicacies sure to satisfy any mood. So, gentlemen, what's your pleasure?"

"Our pleasure?" The question perplexed me.

Gage elbowed me in the side.

"Yes. You're my guest," Dorian said. "You may choose anyone you want. Male or female."

"Redhead," Gage said abruptly beside me. Then quickly added, "Female."

Dorian snapped his fingers, and a pretty, voluptuous, redheaded vampire came to stand next to Gage. He didn't waste any time and swooped her away.

"Don't wait up," Gage called over his shoulder as he let her take the lead as she guided him through a door and out of sight. Relieved that Gage was out of the room and I wouldn't have to deal with his questions until we were back at home, I was still left to deal with my emotions. Gage had never ridiculed anyone for their sexual orientation, but a brother liked to tease, and I had no doubt Gage wouldn't pass up an opportunity like this. However, I also knew he would be rather pissed when it finally dawned on him that I'd fed him a lie all these years about the way I'd been turned.

"Now, it's your turn, my sweet. What type of female would you like?"

I shook my head, still in shock of what he'd become.

"Oh, first, I'd like you to meet my wife."

"Your wife?" Now I was very confused. Why would Dorian take a wife?

"Yes," he lowered his voice and leaned close to me again. "I took a wife for, well, appearance's sake. My lifestyle wasn't always acceptable in society, as you know, and well, taking a spouse was a necessary evil." He laughed, straightening his posture and raising his voice back up to normal. "Darling, come, there's someone I'd like you to meet."

A female wearing a very provocative gown stood several feet away with her back to us as she talked with a small group. Dorian placed his hand on her shoulder as she turned around to face us. "Preston, this is my wife."

Holy.

Shocking.

Mother.

Fucker!

"Lily, this is Preston, my firstborn."

Lily's eyes grew wide.

My eyebrows rose. His wife? Lily? *My* Lily?

She stared at me. Shock mixed with fear coated her eyes. She shook her head slightly in warning when I began to speak. My gaze dragged over her from her face all the way to her bare toes.

Holy fuck! That dress. The starkness of it, the low-cut dip down to her navel, the see-through lace skirt revealing way too much of her. As disturbing as it was to see her wearing something so risqué at a party of Dorian's—no, risqué didn't even come close to what that dress was—my cock grew hard looking at her.

"Nice to meet you," she said, extending her delicate hand toward me. Her gorgeous dark hair was pinned up in some sort of braided concoction, giving everyone full view of every aspect of that dress and what it didn't even try to hide.

"The pleasure's all mine," I returned, taking her hand and pressing her fingers to my lips. I wanted to linger there, pull her against me and away from Dorian.

Dorian. What the fuck was he doing here? I remembered the day he left me. The mixture of fear, hurt, and relief I'd felt when I discovered the note. The amount of reverence I'd felt for Dorian left me confused and full of regret.

"Dorian," I began and then cleared away the lump once again accumulating in my throat. "The way you left was . . ."

"Yes, I'm sorry. I needed to move on. You understand."

No, I didn't. But I didn't respond. I *didn't* understand. I never understood. All I knew was that he'd abandoned me in a small town full of humans with no one else like me around. My feedings had become so minimal, I was lethargic the night I'd stumbled into that bar and met Gage. If it hadn't been for Gage . . .

My thoughts broke as Dorian went on about his party.

"Tell me, Preston, what is your pleasure this evening? Blonde, brunette, or redhead? They're all here for the taking." Dorian's calm voice drew my gaze back to his as he draped his arm around *my* Lily, then placed his other arm around an attractive, no, *pretty* was a better word, dark-haired male standing quietly beside him. The male was clearly under his compulsion the way he stared blankly into space. Except . . . he was a vampire. How the fuck?

Out of the corner of my eye, I noticed another male vampire being ushered from the room, his gaze also blank as though he were compelled. The female leading him away, handed a few bills to Roach as she passed by him.

"So, what'll it be, my love?" The smile on Dorian's pretty face brought back so many memories. "There's no charge for you or your friend. Who would you like to start your evening with?"

A charge? Start my evening? He was nothing more than a glorified pimp. "Dorian . . . I—" I was going to say I didn't understand, but I understood all too well.

"Come on, Preston. I didn't make you a whole man just so you could become celibate. Surely there is someone here who strikes your fancy."

My mind was having trouble wrapping around the situation. Dorian. Here. After all these years. Lily, his wife? My head was spinning with questions.

"You left me." The accusation, the resentment I hadn't known existed, an emotion that had built up in me over the years just popped out without thought. Dorian's eyes snapped to mine, and I ran a frustrated hand over my mouth.

"I left a note."

I laughed. "A note! You left me without any warning!" I shouted. He'd given me a home, showed me affection, friendship. Created a bond so strong it would never leave me. His abandonment created an ache in my chest that I woke up with every fucking evening, not really understanding why it was there. Until now. He'd been the father I never had. Twisted as it was, but a father nonetheless. I blinked at him, desperately trying to clear the fucked-up emotions in my head. No, not a father—a sire. He'd sired me. I wasn't born of his seed, but his blood. He'd made me a vampire.

"You were ready to be on your own. You didn't need me anymore, Preston." He reached up to touch my cheek, but I shoved his hand away.

"You could have talked to me. Let me know your plans. You could have given me time to prepare." Plan for the emptiness that his absence had caused. The ache of the unprepared loneliness that had suddenly overtaken my soul. He'd given me eternal life then left me in a world I didn't fully understand. A world where I knew no one like me, until years later when I met Gage. A friend. A brother.

"I'm sorry. It was wrong of me to leave that way." My eyes shot up and caught his gaze. "You're right. I should have trusted our friendship enough to realize that my leaving that way would hurt you. You needed something that I couldn't give you. You know that. I couldn't stay and watch that side of you any longer. Leaving a note was cowardly of me, I admit, but it was the only way I knew how to handle things because I wasn't man enough to admit it face-to-face."

My heart clenched at his confession. He'd loved me in a way I couldn't return. He'd been hurting. I hadn't considered his feelings. I shook my head, dragging my gaze from his. That Dorian wasn't *this* Dorian. The Dorian I knew was kind and would never hurt or exploit anyone.

What the fuck was I saying? Of course, he would. He'd taken advantage of my gratitude for years. I glanced around the room. Vampires and humans kissing, some publicly fucking. A luxurious orgy. What he was here was no different than a dirty street pimp.

My gaze traveled to Lily's. The light she'd ignited in me stirred in my groin, and I wanted to vomit at the thought of Dorian being with her. But she'd been a virgin. At least there was that. I should have guessed that Dorian would never take a woman that way.

I wanted to whisk her away. Was this why she'd been so hesitant to tell me about herself? She was married to Dorian Spark, my maker, now going by the name Dorian Sweet. Now that she and I had shared blood, I sensed the fear in her.

"What happened to you, Dorian?" I asked.

"I'm the same," Dorian scoffed. "Just wealthier, which happens to most of us as we age and learn the ins and outs after living on this planet for so long. I own Sweet Enterprises. I'm sure you've heard of it. The largest building development and property management firm in the city. I'm sure you've grown in many ways, as well."

"I thought the name was Sweet's Delicacies?" I scratched my head in confusion.

"That is one side of my business. The . . . let's just say . . . the secret side, if you will."

"The illegal side?" I countered.

"Tsk, let's not be a party spoiler and talk of too many business details, Preston. Come now, tell me, son, what's your choice? Blonde, brunette, or redhead?"

I didn't want anyone here except Lily. This Dorian standing before me tonight was not the same Dorian who'd sired me, and he wanted me to choose a sex partner?

I glanced at Lily. Fear evident in her eyes. No, maybe a warning. I was sure she wanted me to pretend I didn't know her; otherwise, she would have greeted me differently. She was not just his wife, she was his whore. No, not his whore. She'd been a virgin. He wanted me to choose a female for the evening? How would he handle me asking for his so-called wife?

"Brunette," I said, staring at Lily.

Dorian followed my gaze. "My wife? You fancy my wife? No, no, no, no, no." He tapped his finger on his bottom lip. "Someone else, Preston. Pick someone else. You can't have my wife. He grabbed a drink from a nearby waiter's tray and downed the green liquid before tossing the glass toward the fireplace. Lily flinched, and several of the guests glanced up at the sound of the glass shattering but then quickly returned to their sexual activities.

Dorian studied me as I gazed at Lily. I couldn't take my eyes off her. She was beautiful. So sexy in that gown. There was a time when Dorian could persuade me to do just about anything. But no longer, and I knew that frustrated the hell out of him. His arm went possessively around her shoulder, and he tugged her closer, but I could see there was no real affection there. Just pride of ownership.

Years ago, there had been times when Dorian would join in with me while I was with a female, claiming that it was always good to share. Though, he never touched them, just me. I wondered how he felt about sharing now. Except I didn't want him anywhere near Lily and me, but there had to be a way to push his buttons so he'd give her to me. He'd always had a difficult time saying no to me.

"You used to enjoy sharing with me, Dorian," I urged, hoping to spark some fond memory of our past so he'd allow me to have her.

His eyes slowly closed and then re-opened. A sign he was giving in. He sighed and released his possessive hold on Lily and then stepped toward me.

"Well, on second thought, this could be interesting." He leaned close to my ear and whispered. "She's a virgin. This is her very first time. You know a virgin's blood is pure and powerful to us. Even vampire blood. And a virgin vampire is very rare, as you know." He winked. I wanted to throw up at the memory. I'd been a virgin when he'd turned me. "And as time passes, the longer a virgin remains pure, the pleasure is said to be insurmountable. I was saving her to turn a huge profit later tonight, but seeing as you're my firstborn, how can I deny you?"

He gently shoved Lily forward, and she stumbled a bit, but I took her hand, steadying her. She glanced back at Dorian, the look shrouded in shock.

Dorian splayed out his arm and waved it toward an open door. "There are private rooms if you prefer. And, Preston . . ." He paused, placing his finger under my chin, commanding my attention. "Take this gift I give you as my apology. I've killed others to keep her pure, as I said, hoping to turn a nice profit. However, I must admit, I cannot deny you." Then he pressed his lips to mine again. I kept my lips hard, my mouth closed, and he pulled away, frustration and anger building in his eyes. But he maintained his composure and backed away.

I led Lily away, my hand at the small of her back as we headed into to a smaller, unoccupied room. There were several rooms with open doors that I figured Dorian had available for couples who required privacy rather than wanting to join in the orgy taking place out in the main room. Not everyone was an exhibitionist.

"Preston. What are you doing here?" she asked, keeping her voice to a whisper when I shut the door and we were finally alone.

"Me? What the fuck are you doing here? His wife? Why didn't you tell me?"

"Please, keep your voice down. I'm sorry I didn't tell you. He parades me around at all his social functions, telling people I'm his wife so they don't find out he's gay."

"What? Why? There's no need to hide that anymore."

"I know, but he's made it clear in the past about who he is. He's afraid to come out now and have everyone call him a liar. He is a highly respected city official and has a reputation to uphold. He uses me and keeps me by his side whenever he attends formal social events. He tells his customers at these stupid private parties that I'm his wife so they won't claim me, but I'm not. I'm his slave."

"Well, I have another word for it. He's a procurer and that, darling, makes you his whore."

She slapped me across the face. "How dare you!" she cried, then ran her fingers over the wetness on her face.

I fingered the sting on my cheek. I should have expected the slap. She didn't deserve that accusation. I knew she'd been a virgin before me. A whore was the last thing Lily was. Plus, I had no right, after all, hadn't I been exactly where she was?

I sighed with regret and reached for her, but she shoved my arm away. "Lily, I'm sorry. You didn't deserve that."

I was still pissed that she hadn't told me, and I didn't understand why she allowed herself to be paraded around at these parties as if she were nothing more than a piece of meat. Why didn't she leave him? No vampire, female or not, should allow themselves to be treated in such a way. But her last words to me as she left my car the last time I saw her reverberated in my head, and I felt like a heel.

# CHAPTER 16

Lily

*P*reston didn't know the half of it. I kept my gaze toward the floor, unable to look at the man I'd fallen for. The sorrow and shame on his face were too much to bear. I supposed in some sense, I was a whore.

Though not for money.

I was a whore to the man who kept my brother captive. I did everything and anything he demanded in order to keep my brother alive. My brother's life was my payment.

"I'm sorry," he said again. I couldn't look at him, but my senses broke loose. The shame he suffered for what he'd called me flowed from him and exploded in my mind. Then he placed his finger under my chin, lifting my face so that my eyes had no choice but to meet his. "I am extremely sorry I called you a whore. You are the furthest thing from a whore that anyone could ever be. And when you left me sitting in my car I was so overwrought with grief and fear that you were in danger. I felt it here . . . inside." He splayed his hand over his chest.

I swallowed the sob in my throat and silently accepted the apology. "Oh, Preston, What are we going to do?"

"First, we are going to do this." He pressed his lips against mine and kissed me slowly, carefully, with such tenderness that I surrendered to him completely. I was his, and he was mine, and not even Dorian—

I tugged away, ending the kiss and he looked at me, his dark eyes glowing with that amber color I loved so much on him.

"Dorian . . ." The name was like tar on my tongue, sticky, black, and disgusting, and I hated that I'd even thought of it at that moment, tainting the kiss that had made me feel cherished and loved. "Dorian has always kept me close, never allowing anyone else to have me. And then, when he's ready to join in the fun, I'm always whisked away to my room by Malik or one of the other vampires he trusts before anyone can claim me."

Preston swiped his hand through his dark hair and bit his bottom lip.

"Lily, why are you here?" His gaze dragged down the length of me. "Wearing this extremely risqué outfit? Why do you allow Dorian to do this to you? You're a vampire. Use your abilities and teleport the hell away from here."

"I can't."

"That's ridiculous. You leave all the time. You meet me at The I.V. You come to my club. What do you mean you can't?"

"You wouldn't understand."

"Oh, believe me, I would. I know the man, remember? He's my maker, or did you miss that part of the conversation out there?"

"No. I caught it."

"So, try me, love. Tell me why you won't leave him?"

I sighed. "He is also *my* maker."

"Shit."

"Preston. I would leave . . . but I can't."

He stood up and walked a few feet away, rubbing his eyes as if they burned, and then turned back to me. "I knew when I saw your eyes. The color when you were with me. I'd seen it before, but I shrugged off the idea. It's the same as Dorian's. The same as mine." He pulled me against him then gently shoved me away, holding me at arms' length. "Okay, that explains why it might be difficult to leave, loyalty to one's maker is a hard thing to deny, but it's not impossible." He placed his hands on my shoulders. "Come away with me. Now. You don't need to be here."

"I told you, I can't leave."

"And the reason you gave me isn't good enough. It doesn't make sense. He's my maker, too. You don't see me parading around in my underwear."

I almost slapped him again for that. But I understood his frustration. I was reticent about the information I was giving him, and he knew it. He had every right to be annoyed with me.

"You know that young male vampire who stood close to Dorian on his other side earlier?"

He nodded. "The vampire with features almost too pretty for a male? The one who seemed compelled . . . which is ridiculous." He waved that last thought away as if it were impossible, which until recently, it was.

"It *is* impossible, unless the vampire is drugged."

His eyebrows furrowed. "What sort of drug would do that to a vampire?"

"More on that in a minute. First, you must know . . . that vampire is my brother."

"Your brother? Lily, how the hell did the two of you get mixed up in this?"

"Let me explain. Dorian and my brother were, at one time, lovers. But when Julian decided he wanted out of the relationship and wanted to explore other options, Dorian didn't like it. So he's been keeping Julian locked up and makes me go out to sell drugs, heroin. He warns me that if I don't return, he'll hurt my brother. Maybe even kill him. If I don't return, he might hurt Julian. Or worse – kill him. I can't take the chance."

"Fucking Dorian. Fucking heroin! You know I hate that shit."

"I know. Believe me, it's not something I enjoy doing. I know that stuff is dangerous."

"That's why you're always hanging out in the Tenderloin? Selling drugs? But I know Dorian. He's not a killer. But he can be rather convincing. No doubt those were all empty threats."

I shook my head. "No. I know how Dorian's hand feels against my face."

"He's struck you?"

I nodded.

Preston's eyes narrowed and I could see anger build from within as his hands fisted by his side. "Fuck! Now, I want to kill him." Then he brought his gaze back to mine and he gently stroked his knuckles down my cheek. "I'm so sorry, Lily. Why didn't you say something?"

"I couldn't. I was afraid. Dorian has been controlling Julian with some sort of drug that keeps him compliant. He's threatened me numerous times and told me that he will kill him if I ever try to escape. He's had us both under his control since he turned us a century ago."

"That's a fucking long time. But I find it hard to believe that he's been drugging someone for that long, especially when I've never heard of a drug with that kind of power. News of a drug with that capability would certainly be known on the vampire circuit after that many years."

"From what I recently learned from Dorian, it's a relatively new drug." I took Preston's hand and led him over to the bed, then sat on the edge and gestured for him to sit beside me.

"I'll explain as much as I can. Dorian only discovered the drug several months ago and has been giving it to Julian. I don't know where he gets it. I've asked around, but no one knows. Until recently, he didn't need it. My brother and Dorian have been lovers since we were turned. *I* stayed because I love my brother. At first, I believed the situation was similar to how you described yours, except Julian returned the affection. They fell deeply in love until . . . I suppose maybe the past few decades or so when Julian's eyes began to wander. He was having sex with females as well as other males. He told me that he was all messed up inside and didn't know what he wanted, just that he wanted to be free to explore. But Dorian found out about Julian's infidelity and killed the vampire Julian had been sleeping with and then locked Julian up, shackled with silver. Dorian kept me because I'd become invaluable to him as someone he could pass off as his wife, and he kept me docile by threatening me with Julian's death if I didn't obey."

Preston sighed. "I'm sorry, Lily. Now I *know* you need to leave with me."

"No. I can't. It's too risky." I began unbuttoning his shirt.

"What are you doing?"

"Taking off your clothes."

"Seriously? We're in the middle of an important conversation."

"Please, I'm afraid he might come in and check on us. We are supposed to be having sex. At least take off your shirt." He did as I requested, and I pulled my gown up, exposing my legs so that Preston could easily slip his hand between my thighs. I grabbed his hand and placed it at my core, and Preston's eyebrows rose at the wetness he found there. I gasped as his finger glided inside me. I hadn't expected him to do that, especially since he'd balked at the idea of getting naked at all. I pressed my hand down on his to stop his movement.

"I thought this was what you wanted?"

"I do . . . but there are things I need to tell you first," I huffed out.

"So, talk." He continued with what he was doing to me, and I had a difficult time concentrating on anything else. There were so many things I needed to tell him, but as his fingers moved inside me, it became impossible to think of anything other than the pleasure building inside of me and the anticipation of having him inside of me again.

"Preston, please, stop. I can't talk when you're doing that."

"I need you, Lily. I've done nothing but dream about you since you left my car."

Knowing that he'd dreamed of me excited me and, suddenly, I didn't want to talk, I wanted to touch him everywhere. The idea of Dorian being just outside in the other room hadn't left my mind. His close proximity ignited a pang of anxiety within me, but I was only doing what was expected of me, after all. He could hardly get upset about that. Just because it happened to be with Preston was the greatest bonus I could have ever hoped for.

I undid the buckle of Preston's pants, and he stood as he shoved them down. He was already so hard. He gently pushed me back onto the bed, and as I lay facing him, his mouth covered mine with a heated kiss. His hand slipped inside the thin, lace bodice of the gown to cup my breast. When he suddenly plunged into me, I closed my eyes at the feeling of fullness, and the prick of his fangs at the vein of my neck took me over the edge of the kind of climax I never thought to experience again.

Press switched from my vein to my lips, allowing me to taste my blood in his kiss. He licked his way back to my throat and sank in his fangs again. As he suckled there, I lost all coherent thoughts of Dorian and Julian. Preston's hands roamed over every inch of my body, and his lips attacked, hot with passion and tenderness. Under him, I came alive and arched up into his thrusts. He was all I could feel, the sensations of me convulsing around him again as he cried out my name, and his heat exploded inside me.

As I lay in his embrace, he held me close and ran his fingers up and down my arm, the motion gentle and soothing. "We have to get you out of here somehow. I had a bad feeling about your situation when you left me, and I searched the city for you that morning. But wherever you materialized to must have blocked the blood bond we'd created. I couldn't track you, and I got caught in the sun. It's taken me until tonight to fully recover."

"You searched for me in the daylight? Why would you do such an idiotic thing?" I asked, stroking my palm over his face, his head, then down to the muscles of his chest.

"I couldn't think straight when you left me. I had no control over what I did. All I could think about was finding you." His voice was thick, still coated with desire. "I couldn't bear you leaving me that way, without knowing anything about where you were going. Don't ever do that again."

"I won't, I promise." I kissed the corner of his mouth. "I'm so sorry you got caught in the sun." Then I kissed his chin and slipped down to his neck to kiss him there. "I didn't know. I haven't even been able to go to The I.V. to see if you were there. Dorian locked me in my room after he discovered I'd been gone all night. He was waiting for me in my room that morning when I returned."

Preston stilled his fingers. "How did he lock you in?"

"I'm not sure. I think there is a spell preventing me from teleporting out of there. When he turns the lock, something happens, and I can't penetrate the walls. That's probably why you couldn't sense me once I entered my room."

"We need to figure out a way to get you out of here. Dorian loved me once. My guess is, he still does; otherwise, I doubt he'd have handed you over to me so easily."

"Maybe, but the Dorian you know, the Dorian Julian and I grew to love and respect, disappeared the night he killed his friend Langdon in a jealous fit. Julian had an affair with Langdon, but in addition to that, Langdon wanted everything Dorian had, including me. When he suggested to Dorian that I live with him, Dorian went ballistic and flew into a mad rage before he severed Langdon's head with this eighteenth-century war sword he has hanging on the wall. I'd never seen anything like that—before or since. It was horrible. I still have nightmares about it. After that night, Julian and I made plans to leave, but it's difficult to escape one's maker when they are so much stronger and find out you've deceived them. Now, he keeps Julian locked up and drugged and uses his captivity against me. Aside from the prostitution, which by the way is a mild description of the business Dorian conducts, he uses me to distribute heroin on the streets. Though he's never used me as a prostitute . . . until tonight."

"Don't think of it that way. You are with me, and Dorian has nothing to do with it. Besides, I would have turned him down if he had offered me anyone else."

"If I don't continue working for him and pretending to be his wife, he'll kill my brother, Preston."

"Then we need to find a way to get both of you out."

# CHAPTER 17

Preston

*I* hadn't slept all day. Leaving Lily with Dorian, tore me to pieces. She claimed to be in danger and I believed her fear was real. She had no reason to make any of that up, except I had a difficult time coming to terms with the fact that Dorian, the man who'd given me a second chance at life, would do her or her brother any real harm. On the other hand, his reasons for turning me had been purely selfish, and he did desert me, leaving me alone without anyone like me, so maybe Dorian was capable of hurting them. As much as I pleaded with Lily to come with me, I couldn't convince her to leave and abandon her brother—no matter how much I tried to get her to understand that I'd find a way to rescue Julian. Now, I needed to find a way to save her *and* her brother. For that, I'd need the help of *my* brothers. Though that would require me revealing the truth about my relationship with Dorian. It was a small sacrifice for someone I cared deeply for. A very little cost compared to what Lily had given up for her brother for so many years.

I didn't even try to go to sleep. Hadn't even gone to my room. I walked through the mansion rather zombie-like. I even hung out in the library for a while and read. Nothing was taking my mind off Lily. I strolled into the studio and played my guitar for a while. Music always soothed me, and I ended up staying in there until the sun went down.

I'd left Dorian's without checking to see if Gage was still there or not. If he was still enjoying himself, I didn't want to rush him. He could take care of himself; plus, he'd already told me not to wait up, which meant he'd find his own way home when he was ready.

I needed his help if I had any chance of saving my woman. I needed *all* of my brothers' help.

When the last of the sun had descended into the horizon, I went upstairs and headed to the living room where I knew everyone would be—a ritual gathering to the beginning of our day that we all enjoyed. I sighed at the sound of voices inside. It was almost time . . . time for me to come clean with everyone.

I walked into the room, and Cian gestured toward the veranda where I saw Gage standing. I knew he'd want to talk to me alone first, and had most likely told Cian to send me outside to him when I got there. I was also positive Gage had already filled everyone in about our discoveries from last night. I tensed a little as I opened the sliding glass door. Gage didn't turn to see who it was, but he knew by my scent. I stood next to him and gazed across the bay.

He handed me a beer he'd had waiting for me, and I grabbed it. I took a swig and let the cool taste of hops and barley coat my parched throat as I braced myself. The dreaded conversation I never, ever wanted to have with him was about to start.

"So, that Dorian dude, I guess you know him pretty well?"

"Yep."

He nodded and took a pull from his own beer. "He kissed you, on the mouth."

"Yeah, he did."

"And you let him."

I inhaled a large breath of air and let it out, then sucked in my lips while I nodded, keeping my eyes on the bridge. The air was warmer than usual tonight for this time of year, and I pulled my shirt off over my head to feel the semi-cool sea breeze. The mixture of salt and mist felt amazing on my overheated flesh after the damage the sun had done.

When I didn't answer, Gage went on. "Don't get me wrong, it doesn't bother me at all. I'm just surprised. I thought I knew everything there was to know about you, but you've never mentioned this Dorian character."

Where did I start? Gage was my best friend. He did know most everything about me, just as I did him. But he didn't know it all, and he deserved to know what had happened. It was supposed to be our pact; *no secrets among brothers* and all that. How had I gone all these years without ever telling Gage the truth about my transition?

"It's complicated," I said.

"No, you know what's complicated, Preston?" I swallowed at his usage of my real name. Gage only called me Preston when he was upset or needed to talk about something very serious. Lane had given me the Elvis nickname, and the rest of the guys had picked up on it. It had all started as a joke at first until Cian had had the great idea to use it in the performance. But it was getting old as far as I was concerned. I needed a change.

I shook my head and stiffened as I waited for Gage to answer his own question.

"If you suddenly lost all your vampire abilities and were dying because you needed constant blood transfusions or something fucked up like that . . . that's complicated," Gage continued. "But fuck, man, telling it like it is? *'Gage, dude, by the way, I like batting for the other team now and again.'* What's so fucking complicated about that?"

"I'm not bi-sexual."

He chuckled, but there was no humor in it. It sounded contemptuous, and the sneer on his face confirmed it. "Yeah? Then what the fuck was that? Why'd you let that fruitcake—and I don't mean fruitcake because he's gay, I mean fruitcake as in he is very weird—play kissy-kiss with your lips last night?"

"I couldn't stop him. Dorian's my maker."

Gage stared at me, his eyebrows knitting together in a mix of anger and betrayal. "No. Wait. You told me that some female vamp named Vicky turned you while you were fucking her."

"I lied."

"You lied? You lied to me?" He was facing me now, pointing his finger at me. "Why would you lie about that?"

"For this very reason. I knew how you'd react."

"I wouldn't be reacting any way if you had just told me the truth from the beginning."

"Told you that I was a cripple, and when the opportunity arose to have a complete and whole life, it meant me being a male vampire's lover?"

"Yes. That." His voice rose several decibels, and he just kept going, hurt and anger pouring out of him. "And you were crippled? Another fact you seem to have left out. You lied to me. And after everything we've been through, you still never came clean. Not until now, until you're forced to. Well, you know what? Fuck you, Preston! Fuck you to hell!"

I flinched as the crash of his beer bottle rang out through the night. I glanced over at the small, semi-circular dent in the wall from where the bottom of the bottle had hit first before the rest of it had shattered into a million pieces of brown glass as it landed on the cement flooring of the veranda. Cian was going to be pissed.

Gage turned from me and stomped back inside; slamming the sliding door closed so hard I thought it might shatter, as well. Then there'd really be hell to pay. But Cian was the least of my worries at the moment. My best friend hated me, and that weighed heavy on my heart. I only hoped that in time, he'd come around and understand why I lied. But now I had to figure out how to rescue Lily and her brother, and it didn't look like Gage would be much help. Apparently, he wasn't as forgiving as I'd hoped he would be.

Seeing Dorian last night had shocked the hell out of me. I'd thought maybe he had died. He'd professed his love to me, but in all these years, he'd never tried to find me again. If he loved me as much as he claimed, I would have thought he'd come back. But now, here he was. And to learn he'd turned Julian so he could be his lover, the same reason he'd turned me . . . Was that a pattern of Dorian's? Changing young men into vampires every few centuries in order to obtain a new lover? And then there was all the drug dealing and prostitution. It seemed to me that Dorian had become a menace to society. Despite the shock, now, the one thing needling the base of my brain was the fact that in order to save Lily, I would need to kill Dorian.

"GAGE DIDN'T SEEM TOO happy when he left," Cian said as I walked back inside.

*No shit. He hates me now, and I need to kill my master, but I'll never be able to do that without Gage.*

I was fucked.

I wasn't even sure I wanted to discuss any of this with them, but if I didn't have Gage, maybe they'd understand.

"Wanna talk about it?" Cian leaned forward, placing his elbows on his knees as he rested his chin on his clasped hands.

I shrugged, and Lane got up immediately, then made a bee-line for the credenza and the alcohol and poured himself a couple of fingers deep from the Johnny Walker bottle.

"Anybody want one?" Lane asked.

"No thanks," Cian said.

"Yeah. I'll take one." Anything to help take the edge off. Alcohol didn't have the same effect on vampires as it did on mortals, but it did provide a generous buzz if we consumed enough of it—without the fucked-up hangover that humans usually experienced the morning after.

"All right." Lane filled another tumbler.

I wanted Gage here, but I doubted he was coming back anytime soon. Dammit. The bastard couldn't forgive me for the lie, and that stung so bad I had a hard time thinking about much else. Gage had been my rock, my one constant through decades of time. My salvation after Dorian had left me alone and lonely in a world full of humans who would never accept me.

I sighed heavily and gulped down the contents of the glass I held. Without thinking, I headed to the bar to pour myself another.

"So, what's this about, Elvis?" Cian asked.

"He prefers to be called by his given name these days."

My head snapped to the doorway where Gage stood. He'd come back. I glanced at the bottle I held, unsuccessfully trying to hide the smile I couldn't contain, and then poured another glass without asking if he wanted it. I picked up both tumblers and headed toward Gage, handing him one. When he accepted it, I said, "Thanks." He nodded and entered the room, finding a seat on the sofa at the opposite end from where Lane sat.

"Preston? Okay. Sorry, man," Cian said.

I shrugged. I'd never told Gage I preferred Preston or Press, but he was good at sensing my feelings. I'd been Press or Preston to him for a while already. He'd never really embraced the Elvis nickname as much as Cian and Lane had. "Whatever you guys want to call me is fine by me, as long as it's not something disgusting."

"Like dipshit?" Lane laughed.

I chuckled. Two seconds later, the rest of the household walked in, including Grayson, Chelle's father, whom I'd requested when I'd told Cian I needed to talk to everyone. The doctor needed to know about this new drug Dorian was using. But I'd forgotten to ask Cian to exclude the women, and when Josh and the other women walked in, I frowned. I hadn't wanted the women here, or the human. Ari was an exception, and was always welcome as far as I was concerned, but Maggie, Vanessa, and Chelle? I sighed. Though the witch might come in handy. But talking about Dorian and my relationship with him was difficult, especially in front of women. Except Lily . . . I suddenly ached to have her beside me. I needed her support. *In due time, in due time*, I assured myself.

Everyone got drinks and sat, waiting for me to start. I glanced around the room and swallowed my pride as I began.

"I'm in love," I started, as claps and *woohoos* permeated the room. I couldn't believe I'd just blurted that out without even considering how it might feel on my lips to say it or how my heart would skip a few beats when the words flowed over my tongue. I *was* in love with Lily. I'd need to be sure she knew that the next time I held her in my arms. I rubbed my hand down my mouth and then took another sip of my drink. I glanced up to see everyone staring at me. Waiting. "But the woman I'm in love with is being held against her will by a vampire named Dorian Sweet."

"Dorian Sweet? The owner of Sweet Enterprises?" Josh asked. Being a reporter, I'd expected him to know who Dorian was. "Fuck. Dorian Sweet is a vampire? He's like, one of the most prominent and influential business owners in San Francisco. Everybody looks up to Dorian Sweet. Just last year, he was voted best in organizational performance by the Golden Gate Business Awards committee as the best in development and construction in the world."

I had no doubt about that after having been inside Dorian's building last night. The place was remarkable.

"That's all true, but he also runs a prostitution and human/vampire trafficking circuit. I did some checking. Turns out, he's managed to tap into a very lucrative niche, one of the largest cartels in California," Gage added, and I was thrilled he was backing me up.

"The victims are usually vampires, but he exploits humans, as well. They are frequently extorted, assaulted, and trafficked for sexual exploitation."

"How the fuck does he compel vampires?" Lane asked.

"Apparently, he or someone else, has developed a drug." I glanced at Grayson. This was his area of expertise. "Once injected into the vein of a vampire, it acts like a roofie and makes them completely compliant, rendering them helpless and vacant. Almost like the sun, but without the pain." Having recently just experienced such an incapacitation, and the calm I'd experienced while unconscious, I completely understood the validity of a vampire's submission under such a drug.

"I may have heard something about this. I'd hoped it was just a rumor, though," Grayson said.

"No, it's very real. It's called Blaze, and I've seen the effects. Gage and I attended a private party at Dorian's last night. Several of the vampires seemed lethargic, some completely incapacitated, but at the time, I didn't realize why until Lily told me about her brother, who is one of the vamps being held against his will and forced to perform sexual acts with both male and female vampires, including Dorian himself."

"The drug was rumored to perform exactly how you described, but also gives a vampire a sense of nothingness."

"That's the feeling I had when I was unconscious due to the sun exposure. After a while, I felt nothing, no more pain, just blankness."

"That makes sense." Grayson nodded. "I'd like to get my hands on this drug. Run some tests. I don't suppose you could . . ." He trailed off. "No. I'm sure you have enough on your mind right now."

"Yes, Lily," I added. "Although she's permitted to leave to deal fucking heroin on the street for Dorian, she is required to return each morning; otherwise, Dorian has threatened to kill her brother."

"She's a drug dealer?" Lane asked.

"Not by choice. He makes her, using her brother against her."

I went on to give them other important information and details about a plan I had for freeing Lily and her brother.

"We'll be there for you. No problem," Cian assured me.

With the plan for rescue approved, tweaked, and everyone's opinion taken into consideration, they all started to get up and leave.

I glanced at Gage. His hard stare penetrated straight through to my bones. I cleared my throat. "There's one more thing I need to tell you all before you go."

They sat back down, eyes on me.

Waiting.

"There's more I feel you should know. I'd rather you all hear it from me than find out any other way." I swallowed. I didn't know why I thought this was such a big deal. Cian and Lane had had plenty of ménages before they settled down with their current love interests. After all, we were vampires, known for our sometimes-eccentric sexual prowess. "Dorian . . . is my maker."

"Ah . . . that puts a new light on the situation," Lane said.

"There's more." I paused to gather my thoughts because this was difficult, not because I'd had a male lover at one time, but because I'd been too weak to stand up for myself. I inhaled deeply and then let it out slowly. No one rushed me. No one acted impatient. They just waited. This was why I loved this family and was so goddamn thankful I was part of it.

"I had a rough childhood, full of hardship and disease. Dorian turned me, made me a whole man when my body was broken and sick. I could barely walk on my own without the aid of a crutch. Could barely breathe most of the time, and had frequent asthma attacks. He promised me a new life . . . on one condition. Dorian took me in not only to give me quality of life, but . . . to be his lover." I glanced around the room. There were no shocked faces. No gasps heard. "He left me years later when it became obvious to him that my sexual preference was females, and he realized I couldn't return the love he had for me . . . at least not the way he wanted. I'm not bi-sexual. I was just . . ."

"We know, El—I mean Preston. We get it. You felt obligated, beholden to your maker. As we all were at one time," Cian stated. "The love we've all had for our sires isn't something we can deny. Not one of us. No one's judging you."

"Does that mean we can't kill him?" Lane asked, and the sound of chuckles burst around the room, giving light to a heavy conversation.

"No. Yes." I hesitated, confusing myself. I knew Dorian would have to die, and I knew I would need to be the one to do it. "I mean, I think *I* should be the one to kill him."

"That works for me," Lane said with a smile. Then he added with a grave, humorless voice so unlike him, "But, if you find yourself unable to do the deed and want me to intervene, don't hesitate to ask."

I nodded as Gage came to stand next to me. "That goes for me, too." He patted me on the back. "I'm sorry I was such a dick earlier. I get why you lied to me, though I don't understand why you felt it was necessary."

"No. I think I'm the one who should apologize. I shouldn't have lied to you. I never liked keeping that secret. I should have trusted you. It was just something I didn't like to talk about, and as long as the topic never came up, I didn't see the need."

"You know I'd walk to the ends of the earth and back again for you, right?"

I nodded again, unable to respond because of the boulder lodged in my throat.

"We're brothers until the end," he added.

"Ah, fuck. Enough with the smoochy, pansy-ass stuff." Lane stood up and walked over to stand between us, draping his arms over both of our shoulders. "Ladies? This is going down tonight, right?" I nodded. I didn't want Lily there any longer than she had to be. "Good. In light of this new intel, my beautiful mate has another idea."

# CHAPTER 18

Lily

"Hey, love." Dorian's all too cheery voice accosted me as my eyes blinked open. I'd voluntarily gone to my room after Preston left. It had taken a lot of convincing to persuade the man that I'd be okay if he left me. Dorian was busy with Julian and everyone else at the party was too involved in his or her pleasurable excitement to worry about where I was. I'd cringed at all the moans and grunts I heard coming from the main room. I hated those parties. I'd always been lucky before, never having to stick around long enough to witness most of what went on at them. "So, how does it feel to not be a virgin anymore?"

I ignored his question and threw back the covers. I was fully dressed in sweatpants and a sweatshirt, having changed out of that hideous gown the moment I returned to my room. I stood, not wanting to be in a prone position while in Dorian's presence.

"You're not happy," He pouted, a childlike expression with his bottom lip sticking out gracing his face. Oh, what I would have given to have the courage to slap it away. "I thought you would be happy. I know for a fact that Preston is a great lover. I assure you, you couldn't have had a better first experience than with him."

I still didn't respond, just walked to the window and stared out at the lights of the city. He didn't deserve to know how wonderful my time with Preston was last night or any other night. He wasn't worthy.

Instead, I answered with, "How is my brother?"

"Oh, he's fine. Lucid even. Would you like to see him?"

I spun around toward him. "Yes! More than anything!" I wanted a chance to talk to Julian when he was capable. It had been so long.

He chuckled. "Fine. I'll take you to him after you tell me how you liked my firstborn."

"He was fine," I said with as little emotion as I could muster. Then added for good measure, "I guess . . . having no one else to compare him to, you know." I knew the minute the words left my mouth that it was a giant mistake.

"I thought you would say that." He rubbed his hands together like he was about to jump into a pool of decadence.

I held my breath.

"Now that you're not a virgin anymore, I plan to use you more often. I'll need to make up the loss of revenue. Letting Preston have you for free was probably a mistake. I could have gotten twenty thousand dollars for you as a virgin. Now you'll need to fuck three times as many to make that up. So many of the vampires have had their eyes set on you. They are all excited to get a chance to experience your beauty firsthand."

I closed my eyes. *Oh, no. Preston, please help me.*

DORIAN LED me to the room where he'd been keeping Julian. I was surprised that he'd let me see which room and where it was. It wasn't very far from mine. All this time, Julian was just a couple doors down from me? I'd had visions of him being in some sort of dungeon, shackled to metal rings embedded into a wall, rats running rampant around him, looking for crumbs. But this room was even nicer than mine. The bed was larger, as big as Preston's. The colors in the room were similar to mine, as Dorian liked red, and I had no doubt that he spent a lot of time in here with Julian. Maybe this was Dorian's room, and Julian just happened to be in it. Oh, no. Maybe he *did* keep Julian shackled up somewhere.

Julian sat by the window, staring out at the lights of the city. I ran to his side, and he glanced at me with a smile. I hugged him.

"Are you okay?" he asked, his concern for me once again igniting a love that would forever burn inside me.

"Me? Yes. What about you?"

"I'll live." He glanced at Dorian then back out at the night sky.

There was so much I wanted to say to Julian. I wanted to tell him that Preston was working on a rescue scheme, but Dorian stood too close, hanging on our every word.

Julian rubbed his hand on his loose-fitting, black silk lounge pants, so similar to the ones Dorian always wore. His T-shirt was clean, and his face smooth from a fresh shave. He'd never really acquired the heavy beard since he was turned so young, so he didn't really need to shave that much. In this moment, he actually looked fairly normal. His coloring was good, too. Dorian must have been happy with his performance last night and stopped drugging him, allowed him the blood he needed to keep his strength up.

"Julian and I have come to an understanding. He's recommitted himself to me once again, and I no longer have to pump that horrible drug into him."

My gaze snapped to Dorian's then back to my brother. Julian nodded as if agreeing, then stood and stepped toward Dorian. I found the shock difficult to hide as Julian voluntarily embraced Dorian, kissing him with what looked like unabashed affection.

What did this mean? Was my brother no longer Dorian's prisoner? What would become of me? When they stopped their public display of affection, I swallowed and found my voice.

"You've forgiven him?"

Dorian smiled, showing his sharp fangs. "When you love someone, forgiveness is easy."

I almost laughed at the absurdity of that statement since it had taken Langdon's life and several decades for Dorian to forgive Julian for that affair.

"What about you, Julian? Have you forgiven Dorian for killing Langdon and keeping you a prisoner for so long?"

My brother glanced at Dorian. "Give us a minute."

My eyes widened as Dorian agreed and walked toward the door. He didn't leave the room, but did give us some space.

Julian took my hands in his and looked at me. My gaze flicked up to his. "I have forgiven him, Lily. And you will, too."

His directness startled me, but I found myself nodding in agreement. "Okay."

This new bond they all of a sudden seemed to share threw me for a loop, but I had to listen to Julian—and trust him. I could never go against his wishes. If he wanted me to forgive Dorian, then I already had.

Just then, Malik poked his head in the door. "Boss."

Dorian walked over, and the two whispered among themselves.

Was this a good thing?

I leaned against my brother, wrapping my arms around him in an embrace. Julian's hand came up to caress mine.

Julian placed his finger under my chin and lifted my face up so that my eyes met his. "You must obey if you want to survive. This is the only way." His voice was low, almost a whisper. "Do you understand?"

"Yes." I'd always done whatever Julian told me to. He was always right. I hugged him close to me. "Julian, I'm working on a rescue. Your plan is brilliant, so stay coherent as much as you can," I whispered into his ear. Julian smiled and gently pushed me away and then stood staring out the window as if I hadn't said anything. His expression blank. His eyes not flinching or making any movement. I walked up close to him again, wrapping my arm around his waist. He didn't move or acknowledge me, but I knew he understood as his hand squeezed mine. If Julian remained lucid, his rescue would be easier.

"Come, love." Dorian's endearing term was a mockery to his actions. He grabbed my arm and tugged me away as I stumbled to keep up. "You have to get dressed. I need you by my side this evening."

"I thought I would be distributing some of the new shipment tonight." I'd promised Preston I would meet him at the bar. I'd been certain that I would be able to get out when I witnessed the arrival of the gang of drug thugs in their black sedans delivering the goods yesterday.

"Nope. There's a charity ball for Alzheimer's, and I'm being recognized as one of the top contributors in the city. Such a nasty disease these humans have to contend with as they age. I do feel sorry for them," he boasted, as if he actually had some semblance of concern for the elderly humans. I knew the truth. The prisoners and slaves he traded in were a testament to his real opinion of mortals.

I glanced back at Julian, who kept staring outside as if he couldn't care less that I was being carted away so abruptly. But I knew better. We had a win today—albeit a small one—and soon, we'd crush Dorian.

# CHAPTER 19

Preston

"Something doesn't feel right," I said to Sting. "Lily should be here by now."

Sting pulled his phone out of his pocket and glanced at it. "Give her another thirty minutes," he said reassuringly before sticking the instrument back into his front jeans pocket.

Two guys strolled in. The same two that I'd seen selling drugs in here before. They sat at the same two stools and ordered the same drinks. A few minutes later, their buyer came in and sat with them. It was like déjà vu as I watched Sting fill first two shot glasses full of whiskey, then a third for the guy with the black hooded sweatshirt.

The exchange of drugs and money happened in the exact manner as it had before. But this time, the one who held the cash pulled out a twenty from the wad and threw it on the table as they all got up and left at the same time. Were they Dorian's dealers? Most likely. He monopolized the drug trade in the city, didn't he?

"You boys stay safe, now," Sting said as he cleared their glasses and swiped up the twenty.

I glanced at my phone. It was getting late. I needed to get to the club. Lily was supposed to meet me here before nine so I could go over the plan with her. If she had a phone, I'd be calling her right now. Last night, she'd been certain she would be given part of the latest drug shipment to sell tonight. Now, I was sick with worry. All sorts of horrible visions flowed through my brain. I wished she'd just left with me last night, though I understood why she didn't. Leaving her brother was not an option.

"Sting, got a pen?"

"Yeah." He snatched a pen from beside the register and handed it to me. I read the inscription on the side. *The I.V. Where blood runs as thick as alcohol.*

I smirked. "Kinda catchy."

He shrugged. "My ill attempt at advertising."

"I like it." I picked up a napkin and quickly jotted down a note to Lily. "Could you give this to Lily if she comes in?"

"Sure." I handed Sting the napkin with my scribbling and stood.

I slipped out the back door and de-materialized backstage at the club.

"You see her?" Gage asked, taking a swig of whiskey.

"No. She must not have been able to get out like she thought."

"Maybe we should postpone," Cian said, placing his hand on my shoulder as he walked by me, his guitar hanging across his back. My guitar, as well as everyone else's, was on stage already.

"Yeah." I knew we should, but I worried about what might happen to Lily and Julian between now and then.

"It's time to go on. El—Preston, do you want to take the lead like we planned, or do you want to wait until the second set?"

"I'll wait. I need to get my head clear if you don't mind."

"Nope. Not at all."

"Love is a tricky bastard, isn't it?" Lane said as he walked by, toting Vanessa by the hand. "We'll take the first number, then."

V stopped in front of me and touched her free hand to my arm. "It will be okay. I have a good feeling."

I nodded and tagged along like a lovesick puppy. Sick to death with worry.

# CHAPTER 20

Lily

I'd taken my time getting ready, trying desperately to figure out a way to leave if only for a few minutes just to let Preston know I wouldn't be able to get to The I.V. tonight. At least not until after the ball, and even then, I really had no idea if I'd be able to sneak out.

As I stepped into the dark red evening gown and struggled with the zipper in the back, Dorian entered my room. He walked to me and turned me around, then zipped up the dress the rest of the way. "It's time to go."

He looked handsome, all decked out in his black tux. A small, red silk scarf the same color as my dress stuck out of his jacket's breast pocket. His hair was slicked back the way he liked it whenever he was in the public eye. His eyes gleamed with a sparkle I hadn't seen in years, and I couldn't help but think that my brother had something to do with that.

"Just one second." I slipped on the silver heels that had been in the box with the dress that Malik had delivered to my room an hour ago. I stood in front of the dresser, wishing I could see myself. Even if I had a mirror, I'd only see an empty room.

All I could do was look down the front of me. The gown was gorgeous. So different than the one I'd been forced to wear last night. This one was elegant, made of red silk, with tendrils of red ribbon curling down the sides to the floor, and not an inch of it was see-through.

Dorian walked up behind me and placed his hands on my shoulders. "I have something for you," he said as he slipped a gold chain around my neck. From it dangled a beautiful red stone. "There. Now you are complete. Here." He held up his cell phone in front of me, tapped the little camera icon and there I was, gazing at myself in the tiny screen.

I looked beautiful.

At Dorian's request, my dark, thick hair had been done up in a weaved chignon with a few stray curls flowing down my neck. No doubt to show off the gorgeous necklace. I fingered the stone, the chain resting so close to the small wounds on my neck that Preston had left so Dorian would know he'd enjoyed me. Then Dorian's tongue ran over the two tiny punctures, closing Preston's mark and making them disappear.

"Though I am pleased to see that my firstborn enjoyed you last night, no doubt leaving his mark unhealed to let me know of his pleasure, I do believe leaving them unattended this evening might prompt too many questions that I'd hate for you *or me* to have to answer. Oh, I almost forgot. Better slip these on your finger."

I hated the rings he insisted I wear each time we attended any type of social event. The too-large diamond set in a circle of smaller diamonds all in a gold setting with a matching gold eternity band of diamonds was a mockery to marriages everywhere. But I let him slide them on over my knuckle.

THE AROMA of fresh roast beef assaulted my nostrils as waiters dressed in black tuxes with white napkins draped over their sleeves delivered the dinner entrees to the tables. Other waiters followed closely behind, refilling wine glasses and water goblets. Dorian sat on my left, and one of the city council members, a large man who smelled of a sweet pipe tobacco, sat on my right. As a plate was placed before me, my fangs dropped in my mouth at the sight of the red blood pooling around the slab of meat on my plate, mingling with the white pile of potatoes. I'd ordered my roast cooked very rare, as did Dorian; otherwise, we couldn't eat it. I closed my eyes and concentrated, willing my canines to retract back into my gums.

The room was spectacular. Several crystal chandeliers hung from the ceiling. I counted ten. There were about thirty round tables in the room with eight guests at each one.

When dinner was finished, dessert eaten, and all the plates removed, everyone was ushered into another room twice the size of the first one. Waiters carried trays filled with cocktails, and champagne flowed from bottles like a stream rushing down a spring mountain. At two thousand dollars a head, I half expected to see diamonds flowing from the bottles, or at least decorating the glasses the bubbly was poured into. I grabbed a flute from a passing tray as I walked with Dorian, my right arm tucked inside his left. I'd say I played my part very well. I smiled graciously when he introduced me as his wife or when someone would approach and tell me how wonderful it was to see me again. I always replied with grace and poise, just as my mother had taught me before she passed from this world. Though I wondered what she would say about all of this.

The room quieted as the MC announced Dorian's name before a boom of applause wafted through the room. As Dorian patted my hand on his arm, I released my hold, and he walked proudly to the podium on the small stage at the front of the ballroom.

I stood alone, listening to his speech. His lies as he promised great things for the charity and told the audience how much of an honor it was to once again earn the recognition from the council for his contributions to such a great cause. I coughed a little, choking on a small sip of champagne. Dorian was a master manipulator, one to be admired, and I suddenly worried about Preston and what would happen if he failed in his efforts to free Julian and me.

After his speech, Dorian rejoined me. Music began, and dancing was the next form of entertainment. Dorian waltzed with me, and graciously gave me up several times when someone begged to cut in. I think I even danced with the mayor at one point.

The night turned out to be very pleasant, in spite of the fact that I was with a monster. Dorian and I stood off to the side of the dance floor when someone, another vampire I recognized from other events, came up and whispered something into Dorian's ear.

Dorian nodded and turned to me. "Let's go."

"But, the party," I complained, finally enjoying a night out.

"You'll like where we are going."

"Where?"

"It's a surprise." He winked. This was a side of Dorian I hadn't seen in quite some time. A playful side. The old Dorian. Had Preston's sudden appearance back in his life sparked something from long ago, making him want to be fun again?

When we reached the limo, the driver held the door open, and I stepped inside. My eyebrows rose at the sight of my brother, dressed in a black tux with a red silk pocket square that matched Dorian's, sitting there. "Julian!" I lunged at him, wrapping my arms around his body.

"You looked lovely dancing tonight," he said.

"You were there? I didn't see you."

"That's because you were having too much fun. I was sitting several tables back. Unless you turned around, you never would have noticed. I couldn't miss Dorian's big night, could I?" he beamed as Dorian sank in beside him and planted a gentle kiss on his lips.

"You should have told me. I would have enjoyed a dance with my brother."

"That would have been grand, though I had to slip out shortly after the meal."

Dorian patted his thigh. "You were perfect."

# CHAPTER 21

Preston

$\mathcal{M}$y head hadn't been into performing tonight. The first half of the night seemed to drag on and on, endlessly. We hung out in the room backstage, drinking and discussing the next set, but I was too worried about Lily to really listen to anyone. Vanessa and Lane had performed another duet toward the end of the first half, and all I could do was wish it was Lily and me sitting at the piano. Though I didn't even know if she could sing, but that didn't matter. In my mind, she had the voice of an angel. I had to blink twice when V's face suddenly morphed into Lily's right there in front of me. I think I actually skipped a few chords.

"Preston.

"Preston!

"Elvis!" I glanced at Gage. I thought I'd heard someone calling me, but my brain seemed numb.

"You okay?"

"Yeah. I'm good."

"Then get your head out of your ass and let's get through this tonight. Okay?"

"Did you just make reference to my brain being *in* my ass?"

"Just seeing if you're paying attention." He laughed.

We headed out of the room in single file. I grabbed the bottle of Johnny Walker from the table on my way. I took a large gulp and put it back, then quickly swiped it back up and took it with me. When I placed it down on the stool behind the piano, Lane grinned. He was always ready for a party.

The lights came on, illuminating the stage and casting the room in front of us into shadows, a blank space of nothing. I knew there were people out there, vampires, maybe even some humans, though, I couldn't see them. When I picked up the acoustic guitar, Cian did the same. Lane sat down at the piano, and Gage laid one of the drumsticks down and picked up the brush for a softer sound. I strummed the first chord of a song I'd written a long time ago. It was a ballad, slower than the rest of the night's selections, but it fit my mood. The words were tender, heartfelt.

Real.

Not something one would expect from me, unless they knew me. I was the shy, quiet one. I was the one who'd frequently cower as a youth, unable to defend himself from the teasing and ridicule of other kids. The bullies that got their kicks out of stealing my crutch and hiding it so I'd have to crawl, dragging the metal braces in the dirt that surrounded my legs as I searched for it. I was the one who'd learned to hide his feelings and refused to show them to others.

Until Lily came into my life.

Dorian had changed me, given me strength. But he'd never been able to tap into that deepest part of me. He'd never penetrated the thick wall I built up. He'd saved me from a life of pain and misery, and I owed him a world of gratitude for that, but I'd never given myself to him completely, not the way he'd wanted.

Dorian changed me physically, but Lily changed me emotionally. Dorian showed me what it was like to be loved, but Lily made me want to love.

The song ended. Applause rang out through the room as the lights came on, and I could see the faces of the audience. As if they'd been pulled by magnets, my gaze landed on Lily's gorgeous face. My heart soared with relief that she was safe. Then it plummeted back down to the pits of hell as I saw Dorian and her brother Julian sitting with her at the table. Dorian's gaze caught mine and held. A grin graced his face, and he held up a glass as though toasting me. I was puzzled about what was happening. Why were they here? Both Dorian and Julian were dressed in tuxes, and Lily . . . Lily was beautiful as she sat on Dorian's left, wearing a red silk gown. I grabbed the bottle of Johnny and unscrewed the top.

"They're here," I whispered to Cian and Lane as I took a gulp. "Lily, Dorian, and her brother, Julian. The one's sitting at the table dressed like they are in the wrong place."

"I see them." Lane picked up his guitar and grabbed the bottle from me. Vanessa was still on stage sitting at the piano.

"Now's your chance for the bet, Lane." She winked.

He grinned and blew her a kiss.

"Stay cool, brother," Gage said as I walked close by him.

Once I was over the shock of seeing the three of them sitting at that table, a song floated into my mind. Like the last one, it wasn't on the schedule for tonight, but we all knew it. There weren't many performances that went strictly by the playbook anyway. My brothers and I were always open to each other's musical needs and talents, and V could easily follow along if needed. I put my acoustic down in its stand and picked up my electric. Taking my cue, Cian grabbed his bass, and two seconds later, I played the first chords of Whitesnake's *Still of the Night* and put on the best show of my life for my maker, whom I was going to kill the first chance I got.

# CHAPTER 22

Lily

The first song Preston had played was moving, and I wondered if he'd written it. The words had been so touching, something I thought he would write. The energy coming from him on that stage was electrifying. When he sank down on his knees and played a solo part on his guitar, I wanted to jump up and dance and scream. Actually, I wanted to tackle him to the ground and have my wicked way with him.

Drinks were delivered, and I sipped at the tequila sunrise—a la vamp—that had been placed before me. A mixture of top-shelf tequila, agave, orange juice, and blood coated my tongue.

I was enjoying myself, though I remained cautious, wanting to keep my guard up. I wasn't sure what Dorian's plans were or why he had brought us to Club Royal. However, I was glad to see Julian enjoying himself for a change. His sudden changes, the renewed admiration he showed Dorian seemed so real. There were several times in the limo where I thought he had true feelings for Dorian once again, and I almost wanted to remind him of the way Dorian had murdered Langdon that night and everything that followed. But now, it seemed like old times.

"He's quite good, isn't he?" Dorian said when the number ended. He reached for his cosmo and held it to Julian's lips for a taste.

My brother sipped and smiled. "Thanks, love. Have you tasted mine? It has cucumber in it."

Dorian giggled and sipped from the delicate, stemmed martini glass Julian held up for him.

They were like young lovers again, and I wanted to puke at the way my brother could ignore everything Dorian had done. But I had to remember that Julian was only playing a role this time. At least, I hoped.

When the clapping settled down and before the next number started, I leaned close to Dorian and asked, "How did you know Preston performed here?"

"Pffft. You insult me, my love. Do you honestly think I don't know where my offspring are? That I cannot track them? Our blood bond is strong. Yes, it diminishes somewhat over time, but the slightest taste renews the bond," he said as he turned to plant his lips against Julian's.

I glanced back at the stage, suddenly remembering the kiss Dorian had given Preston last night when he'd first greeted him. The gentle massage of Preston's finger over his lip immediately after the kiss, the lick of Dorian's tongue over his own, savoring *the* taste.

We'd been stupid to think we could ever pull off a rescue. My and Julian's fate had been sealed that awful night over a century ago. What did Dorian think to gain by renewing the bond between him and Preston?

The band stopped playing, and I wanted to leave. Leave before Preston had a chance to come over to us. I knew he'd seen us. He'd locked eyes with me several times. I had a bad feeling about this night.

# CHAPTER 23

Preston

"*L*et me go alone first, casually," I told Gage and the others. "I don't want anything to seem unusual. Where are the women?" Particularly Vanessa. She'd been on stage earlier performing, but left midway through the second half. If this plan was going to work, we'd most definitely need the witch.

We hadn't planned to do this here at the club, but having the three of them show up so conveniently made a quick change of plans necessary. The sooner I got Lily and Julian away from Dorian, the better.

As I approached the table, Dorian stood to greet me, wrapping me in a warm embrace. "You were very good." His compliment actually settled in and surrounded my heart like a warm blanket. I hadn't realized how his approval would affect me—like a child needs their parent's praise. I needed to get rid of those thoughts. I didn't need him. Dorian was bad news. "Please, join us." Dorian splayed out his hand toward the empty chair between Julian and Lily and then took his place again.

I caught the shy smile Lily gave me, and her cheeks glowed with what I hoped was lust as I sank into the chair, adjusting my now too-tight jeans.

"Hello, again," I said to Lily and then nodded with a smile at Julian. I glanced at Lily and then at her brother, who appeared to be much healthier tonight than he had appeared last night. I wondered what the change was. His dark hair, so much like Lily's, was neatly combed back and hung straight to the top of his shoulders. His brown eyes sparkled, so much like his sister's. But the fact that all three of them were together and looking happy was a puzzle.

What happened to the gaunt, pale lad held against his will from last night? Julian was striking, beautiful for a male, and I could see why Dorian had taken to him so easily. They really seemed perfect for each other. Had they loved one another at one time, like I'd come to care for Dorian? Like Dorian loved me? If I hadn't seen for myself last night the way Dorian treated these two—the blankness in Julian's eyes last night as he'd stood so still beside Dorian, never wavering, the way Dorian had forced Lily to be with me, someone he thought she didn't know—I would almost think they were all happy together.

Then I saw it. It was subtle and under the table, but I saw the flex of muscle in Dorian's arm as his grip on Lily's thigh tightened. The slight wince in her expression as her lip twitched. A reminder from Dorian to be cautious?

Julian stayed quiet beside Dorian. Never giving any indication that he was unhappy or being forced to be there. "We should come here more often," Dorian said.

Julian looked up as Lane approached. His eyes glowed slightly before he caught himself. Vanessa's little idea just might work.

A tumbler of whiskey appeared on the table in front of me as Lane pulled up a chair between Julian and me and grinned. "How's everybody here? Did you enjoy the show?"

Dorian straightened in his seat, his rigid posture suggesting jealousy. Lane *was* pretty hot—at least according to all the women. Julian leaned into Dorian, rubbing his hand up and down his back and placing a gentle kiss on the side of his mouth.

A show of loyalty?

Julian was smart, I decided.

Dorian's shoulders relaxed, and his arrogant demeanor returned. "The show was outstanding. I never realized Preston had that much talent."

"Yeah, El . . . I mean, Preston here is one talented guy."

"What is this El he started to call you, Preston?" Dorian asked.

"They call me Elvis sometimes because of my dark glasses."

"And your name, dude. Preston, Press, Presley. Get it? Oh, and don't forget the way you move those hips." Lane laughed. "Women are all over that shit."

Dorian's eyebrows rose. "I would have enjoyed seeing *that* performance."

I glanced at Lily. She smirked. I'd get even with her later.

"That's right. You and Preston were . . ."—Lane glanced at me and smiled. Oh, he loved this—"roommates at one time, right?"

"Fuck you, Lane," I muttered under my breath so only he could hear me, but that only made him laugh more. I almost laughed myself, knowing it was all just an act. No one could have done this better than Lane.

"Lovers would be more accurate," Dorian stated with an air of confidence eyeing me as he sipped that pink cocktail of his.

"Lovers," Lane repeated, drawing out the word a little too long. "Now that's an *ass* of a different size. So, if you and Preston are . . . Does that mean . . ." He gazed at Julian.

"Watch it, my friend." Dorian's growl skated across the table, jealousy evident in his eyes.

"You just said that you and Preston were lovers."

Dorian's jaw tightened. "We were. You have something against gay men, my friend?"

"No. Not at all." Lane shook his head and grabbed Julian behind the head. Tugging him toward him, he planted an open-mouthed wet kiss right on his lips, just to prove a point—and to not only piss Dorian off but also to rile him up.

I hadn't thought he would do it when he'd joked about it earlier.

Vanessa had bet that he would, and I had bet her a grand he wouldn't. Guess I lost. Julian didn't seem to mind at all and played right into it, completely enjoying the attention Lane was giving him. As I mentioned, Lane was hot, but when Julian's hand came up and tenderly cupped Lane's cheek, surprising the hell out of him, Lane quickly ended the kiss, and I had to stifle my laugh. But Lane was a good actor and stayed in character. Dorian's eyes narrowed at the sensual display his lover had just put on with Lane.

"I don't mind gay men at all. I rather like them." Lane stood and cupped himself. "I just don't like you." He pointed at Dorian.

Dorian immediately rose to his feet. Pink liquid spread over the table as his glass tipped on its side from the abruptness of the motion. Lily and Julian both got up as well and backed away.

"By the way," Lane continued. "I'm not your fucking friend, and this . . ."—he splayed his arms out with his palms open and gestured around the room—"is *my* club!"

Dorian's eyes narrowed. "Is this your doing, Preston?'

I shrugged. "Maybe."

"I misjudged you," he said directly to me with a great amount of disappointment. I couldn't let it bother me. I had to remember he wasn't the same man I once knew. "I thought you would have been glad that I showed interest in your musical talent. I came here tonight in peace. But all I get in return is ridicule from you and your friends. Why?"

"Why?" You want to know why? You're nothing more than a pimp. You hold the woman I made love to captive along with her brother, and I'm supposed to admire you?"

"Do they look like captives?" He pointed at Lily and Julian now, who stood side by side, looking like they'd just attended their high school prom.

They didn't look like prisoners. Not tonight. But I knew the hold Dorian had on them. I understood it better than anyone. "This display tonight . . . you coming here with them like this. It was just a show to make me believe they are happy. But I know the truth. What happened to you, Dorian? What happened to the man who saved me from a life of misery? The sire who loved me?"

"Don't interfere, Preston. You will be sorry."

"Will I?" I glanced around the room and saw that most of the patrons had left, and within a couple of seconds, the rest of my family stood around the table. Vanessa held a crystal in her hand, quietly chanting a spell. Several of Dorian's men stood close by, ready to pounce if anything happened. I'd known they were there, his ever-present guards.

"Face it, dude. You're finished with these two," Lane said, pointing at Lily and Julian. "In fact, you're just plain finished."

If anyone had thought Dorian would show fear or cower in the face of death, they were wrong.

"You are an idiot if you think you can kill me," Dorian said. His eyes darkened, the golden glow that I'd only witnessed during sexual activities appearing with his anger and rage. He flew across the table and lunged at Lane, grabbing him around his throat. The brunt force propelled Lane into the wall, and his head bounced off the hard surface. Lane punched Dorian in the gut, but Dorian was stronger, older. His grip too tight.

One of Dorian's guards came at me before I had a chance to move to help Lane. More guards attacked Cian and Gage. I worried about Lily and wondered where she was, but I didn't have time to stop and look for her.

Gage grabbed the asswipe guard who had his monkey grip around my throat and pulled him off me, snapping his neck. I quickly flashed to Dorian and Lane, grabbing Dorian around the waist and tugging him off Lane. Dorian released his hold, and Lane fell to the floor but righted himself a few seconds later. Dorian turned on me, shoving me back, holding me by my throat now. My feet dangled in the air. His eyes flared with a dark amber hue, a dark shade I'd never seen before, so full of anger it pained me to look at him.

"What happened to you?" I asked again, my voice scratchy, barely audible with Dorian's fingers tightening around my larynx.

"I made you what you are," he growled. "I cared for you. I loved you. Without me, you'd be nothing but a cripple, dead before you even turned twenty-five. Why do you turn on me this way?" he asked.

His tight grip faltered and he suddenly let me go as Julian hit him over the head with a chair. I fell to the floor and regained my stance as Julian lunged at Dorian with a vengeance. I could almost read his thoughts. All the pent-up anger and hatred for the man who'd been his lover for so many years rose in his eyes, bringing about the same golden glow as Dorian's, as Lily's, as mine. I had thought Julian a weak man, but he was proving me wrong as I watched him wrestle with our mutual maker. I glanced around the room. All the others were fighting off Dorian's goons. Chairs were broken, tables toppled over. Even Maggie had gotten into it when another of Dorian's guards had Lane in a headlock. She'd pounced onto his back, choking him while Lane tried beating him off with punches to the face. He finally released Lane, but continued to fight back. Gage was busy several feet away fighting off two of Dorians' guards, while Cian tackled another.

Just as I was about to join Julian in his efforts to subdue Dorian, another guard came at me and tackled me to the floor. In my struggle, I watched as Dorian snapped Julian's neck, rendering him helpless before he plowed into Vanessa, propelling her across the room and into the wall as the crystal she'd held flew in the opposite direction. Though I knew Vanessa's strength could beat most anything, she was no match for Dorian's age and power. The spell she'd been chanting to block Dorian's abilities to dematerialize was instantly interrupted, and she collapsed to the floor. Dorian flashed in front of Lily, and she kicked him in the groin with her pointy-toed high heel, then punched him in the stomach. She looked like a red goddess warrior, but her strength was no match for his either, as he quickly grabbed her around the neck and fisted the pendant she wore, shattering the red gem. Silver liquid dripped down her chest and in between her breasts. Her horror-filled eyes found mine as she collapsed helplessly into his arms. A few seconds later, they were gone. Vanished from sight.

The rage in me grew instantly as they disappeared, and I fought desperately to get to Lily, to follow the bond of our blood before they got too far away. But I couldn't free myself from the weight of two vampires, and everyone was too busy fighting someone else to help.

After too many slugs to my chin, nose, and stomach, my energy weakened as punch after punch pounded into my face and my gut until Gage pulled one of the goons off me. With the weight of just one vampire left, I rolled over on top, effectively giving me the upper hand as I returned some of those punches. The vampire pulled a small blade from his belt and stabbed me in the chest and laughed, showing his fangs his eyes became opaque, leaving only a small black dot of the pupils. The pain roared through me as his hands wrapped around my throat, tightening so I could barely move. I tugged out the knife and slammed it into his throat, twisting it as much as I could. He released his grip from around my neck as his hands flew to his own. I'd had just about enough of this asshole, so I grabbed his head, wrenching it to the side until his neck snapped. I got up just in time to see Gage break the neck of the other vampire, the force turning his head a complete three sixty degrees before slinking to the floor right on top of the other one.

Cian and Lane were busy fighting off two more vampires, but when the two goons realized that Dorian had left, they too vanished from the club.

"Is everybody okay?" Cian asked.

Everyone got up, brushing their clothes and looking around. I did a mental head count as I'm sure everyone did.

"Lily's gone," I huffed out, my breath still heavy from the fight.

Julian had already come to and came to stand next to me, rubbing his hand over the back of his neck.

I swiped my palms over my eyes and down my face and glanced at him. "I'm sorry." I didn't know if I was saying sorry to him or to myself. It didn't matter. We'd lost Lily, my love, his sister.

He placed his hand on my shoulder. "Don't blame yourself. You did your best. Dorian must have sensed something. I don't know how or what. I didn't know the pendant was filled with liquid silver."

"Let's get these guys out of here before they come to," Cian yelled, gesturing to the two vampires Gage and I had just immobilized.

"I have crowd control," Vanessa said and proceeded to work her magic on any humans that happened to still be in the club when all the fighting took place. The rest of the vampire customers had dispersed as soon as the commotion started. Cowards. Though I figured most vampires around the city didn't want to become involved in anything that didn't pertain to them.

I needed to go after Lily and Dorian, but I couldn't sense where they'd gone. I looked to Julian, "You okay?"

He nodded. "Yeah. Thanks."

"Where do you think he took your sister?"

Julian shook his head. "Could be anywhere. I doubt Dorian would take her back to the tower, though. It's too obvious."

"I agree, but it's worth a look."

"I'll go with you," Julian offered.

"No," Gage said. "You've been under his command for too long. You're too susceptible to him."

"But I can help. My bond with him is stronger."

"Dorian's about seven hundred years older than you, and a hell of a lot stronger. If anything were to happen to you, Lily would never forgive me," I said.

"It's better if you stay with us for now," Cian said. "Come back to the house. We have extra space there. You'll be safe and have privacy, as well."

"No kissy-kiss, though," Lane joked. "That, before. That was just for show. Got it?"

"Got it," Julian grinned and licked his lips. "But you are a good kisser."

"Don't I know it." Lane smirked, and Vanessa wrapped her arms around him.

"You were great, baby." She winked at Julian.

# CHAPTER 24

Lily

Silver seared my skin, burning, scorching. It seeped into my pores as it dripped down between my breasts. My limbs turned to rubber, and I no longer had control of them. Though fully aware of my surroundings, I was paralyzed. I'd never been in so much pain in my entire life. I lay on a bed in a room I didn't recognize. A pale blue, down blanket covered the bed. Feminine, lacy, blue-and-yellow curtains adorned the windows. Where was I?

I heard humming from across the room. Dorian? I tried to open my eyes, but it was difficult. Any movement was impossible.

"Please, Dorian," I begged, my voice barely audible. I feared the longer the silver penetrated my pores, the worse my paralysis would become. The silver running through my veins weakened every part of me. My breathing became labored as the metal raced through my body, leaving no organ untouched. My lungs burned with each breath I took. My heart ached with each beat. The pain was too great, and for the first time in my life—human or vampire—I prayed for death to take me, to release me from the agony.

A cool, damp rag covered my chest, and I opened my eyes just enough to see Dorian wiping the silver off, but it was too late. The poison was already in my system, wreaking havoc on every nerve, every bone, every muscle.

"This should help, or at least prevent more from entering your body," he said as he continued to rub the silver from my skin. "Though I'm afraid the toxins will stay in your system a lot longer, but that is unavoidable." His hands were covered with plastic gloves to prevent him from touching the metal. "I had a feeling you and Preston were concocting something stupid. That's why I had you wear the pendant filled with pure liquid silver tonight. The cheap garnet kept it safe from harming you until I broke it." He tapped the side of his head with his finger and winked. "Brilliant, don't you think?"

Why had he taken *me*? Not that I wanted anything bad to happen to my brother, but I figured Dorian would want him more than me. I'd always been just an ornament; someone to parade around at social gatherings so city officials and other important people wouldn't know Dorian was gay. Someone to deal his drugs. It was my brother Dorian had coveted for so long. Though in this day and age, homosexuals weren't blackballed the way they used to be, and vampires could care less. Many vampires had sex with both genders all the time. It wasn't anything to be ashamed of, yet Dorian was.

"Why?" I croaked out.

"Hmmm? What's that, dear?" He lowered his head closer to my face. An inch closer, and I could have bitten his ear off if only I could have made my mouth work better.

"Why me? I thought it was Julian that you wanted so badly."

"Yes, well, I still need you. Without you accompanying me, people will start to question my validity as a good business associate. My standing in this community means everything to my investors. If they lose faith in my commitment as a loyal and dedicated husband and family man, I lose them. As long as I can keep convincing them that I am a devoted husband, ready to start a family, they trust me. Don't you see? If they knew the truth, I'd be labeled as a liar, someone without integrity, and no one would trust me anymore."

"What about Julian?"

"Julian will return to me. You just wait and see. As long as I have his sister"—he touched his finger to my nose in a playful way. His ill attempt at being cute, I supposed—"he will come back. We just have to give it some time. I bet by the time we get back home after all this nonsense blows over, Julian will be there waiting for us. "

"But why would you want him if he doesn't want you?"

"He *does* want me. Of course, he wants me. He's just playing along with Preston." Dorian continued to wipe the cloth over my chest. The beautiful red gown was ruined. He'd torn it at the bodice in order to clean up the poison he'd let flow over my skin, and the ragged material frayed and covered with silver spread open, exposing my breasts. As long as the liquid metal stayed on me, I would never heal. "Julian knows what to do, and I'm sure he's doing an excellent job playing the poor, defenseless, and abused gay vampire for Preston and his bandmates."

Dorian was delusional. Hopelessly blind to how my brother really felt about him. Julian may have fallen in love with Dorian years ago, but after Langdon's murder, after all the years of abuse, I was positive that the hatred my brother harbored for Dorian was much greater than any love he may have had for him in the past.

I had to try to get a message to Preston. I only hoped that enough time had passed since Dorian and I exchanged any blood, or that bond would interfere.

"How can you believe that? You saw the way he returned Lane's kiss. Do you really think he would have done that if he loved you?"

The minute the words left my lips, I knew I'd gone too far. Dorian's open hand slapped me across the cheek with such force, the inside of my mouth stung, and I could feel my teeth shift in my gums. Tears sprang to my eyes. I still couldn't move, and I desperately wanted to rub the side of my face.

"Don't make me punish you. Julian was being polite. That's all."

I would have laughed at the absurdity if I could have.

I managed to lift my head a little and looked around the room. "Where are we?"

"You don't think I'm going to tell you, do you? Trust me, we are far enough away that your bond with Preston, and Julian's bond with me will never help them find us. So, for now, we are safe. Once this all blows over, we'll go back to the tower and resume our lives. There. All the silver is gone from your chest now. We do need to get that dress off of you, though." Fisting his gloved fingers around what was left of the bodice, he yanked until the entire dress was ripped down the front. He tugged it from beneath my body and tossed it in the corner of the room, leaving me naked and feeling even more vulnerable.

# CHAPTER 25

Preston

*D*orian's tower suite was vacant, just as Julian had thought. Not even his henchmen had stuck around. Gage and I searched the entire building, looking for some clue as to where Dorian would have taken Lily to hide. By the time we finished, there wasn't a piece of furniture that wasn't upended or a drawer not emptied with its contents on the floor. Every piece of paper had been read, every cabinet searched, every picture taken down from the wall to check for a hidden safe. But the only things we'd come up with were a metal box holding a plastic bag of something we assumed must be the Blaze drug, and a couple of vampires held captive by silver shackles that we had to use an old hatchet on to remove in order to set them free. We found nothing about where Dorian could have possibly gone with Lily. Chances were, he hadn't come back here first before taking off.

What had happened to Dorian? I kept asking myself that question over and over again. He was not the same vampire I had lived with for so many years. After setting the vamps free, I righted one of the red velvet-covered armchairs and sat in it. Gage did the same, but not until he helped himself to some more of the absinthe that had been sitting in a carafe inside one of the cabinets. He offered me some, but I declined. I wasn't a fan of the stuff, to be honest. Plus, I was exhausted. I think we both were as we sat for a while, not having any clue as to where to search next. Gage drank his green shit while I worried about Lily and where Dorian had taken her.

This furniture was hideous. Fucking red velvet all over the place. I ran my hand over the soft fabric. Dorian always did like soft material, décor with a feminine flare. But not to this extreme. Not stuff that looked as if it belonged in a bordello. He'd fancied lace and crocheted table toppings, if memory served. And pretty pastel bedding. My eyelids stung from worry and stress, so I let them close to combat the sting as a memory floated into my mind.

*THE LIGHTS IN THE SMALL, quaint room had been turned down low. Fire crackled in the hearth, and I sat close by, huddled in a soft, white wool blanket, naked underneath, in an attempt to warm my chilled-to-the-bone body. My rain-soaked clothes hung to dry on a rope he had strung from two chairs positioned on the other side of the fire. My body shook, still too chilled to move. My leg ached from the cold, my joints inflamed with arthritis, and I winced as I tried to shift in the chair to ease the pressure on my hip. My brace lay in a heap on the floor next to me, the metal rusted from years of wear and tear, though it was all I could afford. At the young age of nineteen, I hadn't worked at the school for very long, and medical equipment like leg braces was expensive. The one I owned had been provided by the orphanage I'd grown up in. It was old, and the hinges were corroded. This rain would make it worse, and my ability to get around even more difficult.*

*He handed me a small glass filled with something dark and golden brown. I sniffed at the glass. "What is this?"*

*"It's brandy. Drink it. It will help warm you. My name is Dorian Spark, by the way, and this is my home."*

"Tha . . . thank you," I stuttered from the chatter of my teeth. "I'm Preston Knight."

I tasted the foul-smelling liquid and swallowed some as the burn coated my throat, but it did as he said it would. With each sip, my body grew warmer. When I'd finished the entire glass, he poured me another and gave me some warm chicken broth.

"I don't have much in the way of food," he said. When I gave him a puzzled look, he added, "I don't require much."

"Thank you," I uttered in a soft, cautious voice. Grateful for what he offered, yet the puzzle of our arrival here in his house was still a mystery.

"What is wrong with your leg?"

"I was born this way. They never gave it an actual name, and the cause for it was deemed inconclusive."

He nodded. "How old are you, Preston?"

"I'm nineteen. You?"

"Let's just say that, for all intents and purposes, I'm twenty-three."

I thought about that for a minute, not sure what he meant by it, but being as polite as I could be, I didn't question him. Either you were twenty-three, or you weren't. My guess was that he was older but didn't want to let on. Some men, I supposed, were vain about their age.

"Where are your parents?"

"Don't have any. I grew up in Saint Mary's Orphanage; the one by town hall," I said, not really knowing what town we were near, but with any logic, it seemed we would have to be close to the school I taught at.

"Yes. I know of it."

I had to admit, he was a handsome man. His long, dark hair was neatly combed and tucked back behind his ears. He had no facial hair concealing his smooth, unblemished skin. He seemed very refined, somewhat graceful even. He must have grown up in a very wealthy home, and I suddenly felt unworthy of this new friendship I found us developing. With the help of his charm and the brandy, I'd succeeded in shrugging off the low self-esteem that had plagued me my entire life and ignored the voices in my head telling me I wasn't worthy.

I finished the broth he'd given me and set the bowl on the table to my left. Then I drained the contents of the second brandy before he poured me *another. I wasn't used to drinking, but the effects were dulling the pain in my leg and continuing to warm me up and make me feel more at ease, so I drank it. And when he offered me another, I drank that, too.*

*"Preston."*

*I glanced at Dorian and grinned. He smiled back at me, and my vision blurred a bit. "What would you say if I told you I could heal you? Rid you of this awful disease."*

*I laughed and then quickly restrained myself at his somber expression and realized my rudeness. "Are you a doctor?" My question, of course, was ridiculous, considering his age.*

*"Hardly," he admitted and sipped at his own glass of brandy. "But I can heal you. In fact, not only can I heal you, but I can give you eternal life."*

*I rubbed my ear, thinking I hadn't heard him correctly. The effects of the booze must have been making me hear things. The absurdity of his claim was too farfetched to be believable.*

*"I only ask one thing." He paused and tipped my chin up with his finger so that our eyes met. The golden glow mixed with the dark brown surrounding his pupil was beautiful, but I had to look away. And then his hand slipped to my thigh. He ran his tongue over his lower lip and then pressed his mouth gently to mine. I wasn't the type of man that I suddenly realized he was. Though his offer to heal me had intrigued me, and I wanted to hear more. I was willing to do almost anything to be rid of the pain I'd had to endure my entire life.*

*Though his comment about eternal life still was not clear, I shoved that idea to the back of my mind and focused only on the part about me being a whole man instead of the cripple I was. With that thought firmly in mind, I allowed him to kiss me and found it less uncomfortable than I had expected.*

*"I will do whatever you ask," I said against his lips.*

*He smiled and tipped my head to the side, and I gripped the fabric of the armchair as he consumed a part of me that would never resurface. My humanity.*

"PRESTON!

"El?

"Preston! You okay?"

I opened my eyes to see Gage looming over me as if I'd been out for hours.

"I'm fine. I must have fallen asleep."

"I'll say. You were talking gibberish and fidgeting in your seat over here. Come on. We need to get out of here before the sun comes up." He frowned and studied me for a moment. "You okay?"

"Yeah," I lied, willing away the haunting memory of my past as I released the death grip my hands had on the side of the chair as something clicked in my brain.

I stood and glanced at Gage.

"I think I know where he took her."

# CHAPTER 26

Lily

*I* floated in and out of consciousness, still unable to move as the silver flowed through my veins, tainting the little blood I had left in them. I desperately needed fresh blood. I lifted my head a little, just enough to peek at my surroundings again. I tried to place the unfamiliar antique furnishings, but nothing came to mind.

I concentrated on trying to transmit a message to Preston through our bond. I wasn't sure if it would work, but I had to give it a try. I did know that if he were close enough, he'd be able to sense where I was. There was no sign of Dorian in the room, though I had the sense that he remained close.

I closed my eyes, wishing that I could help my blood replenish itself on my own, but I knew I'd need to ingest some in order for that to happen. A welcomed sleep took hold.

. . .

*"DRINK, LILY." My brother's voice was so clear in my head, yet so distant. "You'll need to drink if you want to survive. He pressed something warm to my lips. It tasted of copper, and it was nasty, but once I swallowed it, the flavor changed, and my taste buds craved more. I sucked hard at whatever it was that Julian pressed against my mouth, drawing out as much of the liquid as possible. "That's it. This is what you need to live." Julian's voice was soothing, and I opened my eyes to find his beautiful dark ones gazing into mine.*

MY EYES FLICKED OPEN.

What a strange dream.

I heard someone whistling an old tune, one from years ago. The sound became louder as Dorian entered the room. He had a bag of blood in his hand, and he sipped at it. I licked my lips at the delicious smell. Was he going to give me some?

"I heard you call out for your brother. Don't worry, he will be here soon, I promise."

"No." I shook my head slowly from side to side. It couldn't be true. It was only a dream. This was all too cruel. It was the lack of sustenance playing tricks on my mind.

Dorian grinned as he sipped on the straw protruding from the bag. "You probably would like some of this, but then you'd get stronger, and I can't afford that."

"Dorian, please," I begged. The scent of the blood, the much-needed nourishment, teased and tormented my senses. My arms barely twitched as I tried desperately to move them.

"No, I'm sorry, you need to stay incapacitated for a little bit longer. But Julian will come. He will come for you, I have no doubt. A brother's love for his sister is strong. And I have to admit, your brother's love for you is unusually strong. A love I could never quite understand, nor a bond I could sever." He made some tsking noise with his tongue. "Though I tried several times, believe me. You've been nothing more than a nuisance, a huge inconvenience as far as I'm concerned. Sure, yes, you've come in handy with my career—which I am grateful for, mind you—but your existence has done nothing but interfere with my relationship with Julian. I came *this* close,"—he held his forefinger and thumb a quarter inch apart in front of my face—"so many times to killing you. But Julian would never forgive me for that. That's why I agreed to keep you alive all those years ago. So, my dear, here we are. Waiting."

My body replete in misery, I closed my eyes.

What hell was I in?

# CHAPTER 27

Preston

𝓘 stood in the room where Lily had stayed when she was with Dorian, the color red prominent even in here, though this room was adorned with silk rather than velvet. I envisioned her sleeping all snuggled up under the soft silk spread covering the bed. I needed something of hers. Something imbrued with her essence.

As I stood over the bed, something caught my eye. Something dark blue, sticking out from under the pillow. I reached under the cushion and picked up *Interview with a Vampire*. I remembered her telling me about loving romance and erotica novels.

I found one of those reusable, canvas tote bags in Lily's closet and shoved the book inside, throwing the strap over my shoulder.

I wanted to confirm my suspicions about where Dorian had taken Lily. The chances of the house of my second birth still standing were slim at best, and I needed Vanessa's help in order to see if she could conjure a vision. I'd need to form a plan of attack and not just appear inside when I didn't know what he had in store. Dorian was a clever vampire, and I had no doubt there would be a trap of some sort.

Everyone sat in the large living area when Gage and I returned. Julian stood the minute we entered the room. "You didn't find them." It wasn't a question, but I shook my head anyway.

"I think I know where they are, though. Vanessa, I need your help." I pulled the book out of the bag. "Do you think you could use this to conjure a locator spell?"

She stood and walked to me and took the book. "I should be able to. This is Lily's?"

I nodded. "And if you can somehow see the place, the surroundings would be helpful. I don't want to walk into a trap."

"Good plan," Lane said.

"Start searching in Louisiana and the surrounding areas. I'm working from memory, and unfortunately, that area isn't anywhere near the same as it was." I only wished I could remember exactly where, but too many years had passed, and for all I knew, changes to the land may have even destroyed the place. Hell, Louisiana wasn't even a U.S. territory yet back then. Honestly, I'd be damn surprised if the property still existed.

"I have to go with you this time, and I won't take no for an answer," Julian said. "It's my sister he's holding captive."

I didn't respond, but I didn't argue either. No one did. It was his neck, and he was right, she *was* his sister. We had no right to keep him from helping. I strolled over to the credenza and poured myself a drink, letting the burn of the scotch coat my throat as I glanced through the see-through one-way glass as the morning's first sunlight glowed upon the hills on the other side of the bridge.

Julian stood in front of the windows looking out. Shielding his eyes, he stepped back a few feet. He stilled when he realized he would be okay. "This is amazing. I haven't seen the sun in over a century."

Everyone got up and joined him at the window to stare at the sun. It had become a morning activity that we all enjoyed.

"We had these windows installed a few months ago. We still

haven't gotten tired of admiring how the sun ignites the sky from behind us and watching it set in the afternoon," Cian said.

"It is amazing. One of the only regrets I've ever had about becoming a vampire," Julian said. "Well, aside from the last couple of decades of being held against my will. But Dorian wasn't always a monster." He glanced at me. "I'm sure you remember a much different man than the one you know today."

I nodded. "Yes. What happened to him?"

He shrugged. "Love. Jealousy. Greed. He became obsessed with money, though he never had the patience to acquire it legally. He and I began peddling opium and morphine in the early nineteen hundreds to the sick and injured, then moved on to heroin and cocaine in the early twenties a few years after they became illegal. In the eighties, I told him I wanted out. That I didn't want to push drugs anymore. He wouldn't listen and just ignored my wishes. I stopped helping him and because of that, he was never home anymore. I told him I was taking my sister and leaving. I'd had an affair with someone who'd ignited the spark that was missing with Dorian and in a jealous rage, Dorian murdered him. I'm not saying what I did was right or how Dorian handled it was right or wrong, but since then, he's kept me under his control, lacing me with silver, depriving me of blood, and now, recently, injecting me with some drug he calls Blaze. My sister only stayed because of me, and now her life is in danger. I can't just sit back and let someone else rescue her."

"Tell me more about this drug," Grayson said as he put his arm around Julian's shoulder and led him over to the sofa for a more in-depth conversation.

I TRIED to sleep but ended up tossing and turning too much. I drank some blood from the fridge. Three bags, in fact. I wanted to make sure I had enough strength to deal with Dorian. I wasn't sure how Julian would handle himself, but I had to trust that he loved his sister and wouldn't do anything to mess up the rescue.

As I lay in my bed, I tried to concentrate on Lily. Though we'd exchanged plenty of blood, my efforts were futile. My only hope was that Vanessa would be able to locate her with a spell.

After the sun had gone down again, I strolled into the living area and everyone was already there. Lane stood next to Vanessa, and she smiled at me as she held the book against her chest.

"You found them?"

She nodded. "Yep. And Lane found the property using Google Earth so you can get an idea of the surrounding area and how to approach the building. It's an old stone house, off the beaten path, and hidden among a patch of trees. Very secluded."

"Yes. That's the same as it was. I'm surprised it's still there."

"So you know the place?"

"It's where he turned me. I just couldn't remember exactly where it was."

"That's an awfully long way for a vampire to travel, especially toting a disabled and helpless female," Cian said.

"Unless they flew," Julian spoke up. "He has passports for travel. We all do. And if he had her in a wheelchair, the airlines would have accepted them."

I sighed.

"Looks like we're going for a plane ride," Lane said with a wide grin.

"Why would you come?" I asked.

"We're all coming," Gage said. "No way are we letting you tackle this dude on your own."

"Even with Mister Kissy Face here, that's not enough. You need us," Lane added, pointing his thumb at Julian before quickly wrapping his arm tightly around Vanessa and tugging her against him. He'd had some issues not too long ago, issues pertaining to some abuse he'd endured as a kid, and I had to wonder if his little show with Julian last night had affected him in any way. But as long as he was able to crack a stupid, insulting joke, I figured he was fine.

# CHAPTER 28

Preston

We had to book an evening flight out of San Francisco International with a two-hour layover in Los Angles. Why we had to fly south for an hour to go east for four was beyond me, but I was thankful that the plane wasn't very crowded and that Cian had managed, with a bit of compulsion, to acquire first-class seats.

I almost felt sorry for the poor first-class human ticket holders that had lost their seats to a last-minute emergency Vanessa had conjured as an illusion. But, hey, they could travel at any time of day and would be able to catch the next available flight. And this *was* an emergency.

The flight attendant brought me a scotch, and I tried like hell to relax. I wasn't afraid to fly; I was just worried about Lily and what Dorian was doing to her. But considering who he was, I at least knew he wouldn't sexually assault her. Though he could be rather mean and hurt her in other ways.

The coincidence of Lily and I having the same maker, and her brother also being of the same blood hadn't escaped me. But I considered it a plus. Dorian might have changed over time and may have coveted all the wrong things in life, but I didn't think he had it in him to kill one of his own. Harm yes, but not kill. At least, I hoped not. I knew what I had to do, though, and it bothered me a great deal. I hoped that when the time came, I'd have the courage to go through with it.

Killing Dorian would be the hardest thing I'd ever have to do.

I sat next to Julian. He'd been chewing on his fingernail when a male flight attendant stopped by to see if we needed anything.

"You boys okay?" he asked, and Julian looked up at the guy as they gave each other a sexy smile.

Shit.

"Maybe a couple more scotches," I said.

"Will do." He gave Julian the once over before leaving to retrieve the drinks.

"Do you have to do that?" I asked.

"Do what?"

"Flirt with the attendant."

He smiled. "I've been locked away for some time. Don't begrudge me this one tiny pleasure. You're looking at the new Julian. This is only the beginning of what I foresee as a very enjoyable future for myself."

I nodded. How could I deny that?

The attendant placed the drinks down on our trays. "Thank you," Julian said, brushing his fingers over the back of the guy's hand as he let go of the plastic cup. The attendant winked at Julian and sashayed away.

I glanced at Julian. His brown eyes glowed with the same amber color as mine.

"We have the same eyes."

"What?" he asked as he sipped his drink.

"Our eyes. Yours, mine, and Lily's. We all have Dorian's glow when we're . . ." I worried about using the term with her brother, but what the hell. "Aroused."

"Yes, though Lily's eyes are not Dorian's."

"Of course, they are. That glow is unmistakable. They're just like ours."

"Mine. They are just like mine. I am my sister's maker."

My eyes widened. This couldn't be true. "What are you talking about?"

Julian chuckled. "My sister. I am the one who turned her. Therefore, she has my eyes, not Dorian's."

"*You* turned her?"

"Yes." He took another sip of that stupid drink, and I wanted to choke him.

"Why would you turn your sister?"

"It was either that or watch her die. I love my sister, and I couldn't imagine life without her. I couldn't let her die. We're not even a year apart in age. We've always been close."

A part of me was pissed that he'd done that to his sister, but then another part of me was grateful. Grateful on two counts: one, that he'd saved her from death; and the other, that Dorian wasn't her maker and she was never actually devoted to him, but to Julian.

"What happened?"

"Dorian drained her of too much blood while I was in transition. He was going to let her die. But then he realized that I would hate him for that, so he allowed me to turn her."

"The bastard." The hatred building up inside me for Dorian was growing by the hour.

"I would have turned her anyway. If Dorian hadn't bitten her, I would have. I didn't want to live an eternity without my sister."

I nodded because, on some level, I understood. I also understood the influence Dorian could have on someone.

"Did you let Dorian turn you, or did he force himself on you?" I had to ask because it made a world of difference to me.

"A little of both, I suppose. He seduced me. He was very charming, and I fell instantly in lust with him. Then, during the heat of the moment, he bit me. At first, it frightened me, but the longer he sucked, and the longer he fucked me, it turned into the most blissful experience I'd ever had. Granted, I was young and didn't have a lot of experience. Any, in fact. I was a virgin." He laughed and finished his scotch, then wiped his mouth with the napkin. "But *force* wouldn't be the term I'd use. After he'd had his fill and we both climaxed, I wanted more. I asked for him to turn me and promised to be his lover."

I was no one to judge Julian. But Lily hadn't asked for any of this.

"This is not the same story your sister tells."

"Don't blame her. She has a somewhat . . . distorted memory of it all. She was under Dorian's compulsion the entire time and was left to sit in the other room reading while we were . . . engaged. Julian paused for a few seconds to glance out the window as we passed through a blanket of clouds, and the plane rocked a bit with turbulence before settling down once more.

"When Dorian approached me," he continued, "I was instantly attracted to him. As I said. The lie he'd told me about why he—a stranger—was even in our house seemed believable at the time. He'd claimed to be a friend of our father's. I had no reason to not believe him. He never needed to use his compulsion on me, and I hadn't given a thought to Lily's whereabouts. I was barely nineteen and very sexually curious."

I grabbed my glass and drank down the remainder of my scotch. Though I'd been the same age as Julian when Dorian turned me, I hadn't thought much about sex back then. Perhaps if I'd been a normal teenager, I might have given in to the lure. But being a cripple, no woman had ever looked at me twice. And I was never attracted to men. The promise I'd made to Dorian to be his lover if he cured me had been done simply because I couldn't stand myself any longer. I hadn't realized the impact of it all at the time. Back then, I'd been too enamored with the idea of living life without sickness, and I didn't care what I had to do to achieve that. Once I'd been made whole and grew into my body as a strong, virile male, my new muscles infused with their vampire strength, women paid more attention to me, and I liked it.

The plane landed with a jolt, and it startled me since I'd paid little to no attention to the captain's announcement that we would be landing soon.

We piled out of the plane and then into two separate taxis. There were seven of us as Maggie had insisted on coming along as well, though no one expected her to fight. She was small but strong and could certainly hold her own if ever accosted by a human, but not against a seven or eight-hundred-year-old vampire. Hell, none of us except Gage were even in the same league as Dorian.

I sat in the backseat of the taxi, Gage on one side of me, and Julian on the other.

"How old are you anyway?" I asked Gage.

He shrugged. "Lost count."

"Take a guess." Julian prodded, sounding very curious.

Gage frowned and glanced at me. "I've never told you?" He picked at a frayed edge of the fabric bench seat we sat on in the back of the taxi.

"Not that I can remember."

"I'm sure I told you."

"Just tell me now. I want to know if you're older than Dorian."

"How old is he?"

"I'm not sure. Seven or eight hundred years, I think." I kept my voice low so the driver couldn't hear and gave Julian a glance as he nodded in agreement.

"You don't have anything to worry about," Gage grinned.

WE PULLED off the main highway onto a dirt road, and I instructed the taxi driver to let us out along the shoulder. We made sure that both drivers were compensated for their time and bid them on their way, their minds gently altered just in case. My memory of the area was returning, though so many things were different now. I could only guess that we were about a mile out from the house. A part of me dreaded returning there. The thought of seeing the place, the memories I knew would surface, I didn't want to think about them.

The group separated, and I traced my way to the side of the house while the others hung back, including Julian. I was surprised the original brick still appeared intact, though the building looked much smaller than I remembered. I flashed to one of the side walls, and Gage materialized a few feet away to my left on the other side of another window. I peeked inside. It was the main front room of the house and gave way to the open kitchen on the other side. The room where I'd been given eternal life. I closed my eyes as the memory of that day flooded my mind, swamping me with all sorts of emotions I didn't need right then. I blinked and rubbed my eyes. Gage gave me a silent *what's wrong* look, and I shook my head. Then he pointed at the window he stood by. It was the bedroom, and he nodded with a smile, mouthing Lily's name. A river of relief flowed into my heart with the knowledge that she was still alive.

I heard a crash from inside and glanced in through the window. I saw Dorian standing by the kitchen counter. A pile of broken glasses mingled with broken dishes lay scattered on the floor in front of him. He lashed out as more dishes went flying and he cursed. His anger was building about something. Did he somehow sense we were there?

We hadn't been able to take any weapons on the plane, and I hoped I'd be able to find a blade inside that would be sharp and large enough to do the deed. I motioned to Gage that I was going in, and he nodded. This was the plan. I'd go in first and act as if I'd come alone.

I materialized on the other side of the kitchen counter from where Dorian stood.

Sensing me, he turned and glared at me. His eyebrows pinched closely together.

"Preston."

"Dorian," I returned.

Glad to have the brief exchange of pleasantries out of the way, I asked, though I already knew the answer, "Where's Lily?"

He ignored my question. "I knew you'd find me here eventually if I gave you time. I'm impressed you got here so soon."

"Where is she?" I asked again.

"She's in the bedroom. She's fine." He waved his hand in the direction of the room, and I took a couple of steps that way, only to find Dorian in my path. "No. You can't go in there."

"Why are you doing this, Dorian?"

"I'm sorry you had to get mixed up in this, Preston. I've never stopped loving you, you know. It breaks my heart that you became involved with any of this."

"With this? That's *my* woman you have in there."

Dorian's eyebrows rose. "One fuck and now she's your woman?" He laughed. "Preston, I'm surprised. I gave you more credit than that. You can't seriously be in love with Lily after only spending one night with her." He sighed a heavy breath. "And I'm so sorry about that, but she belongs to me. At least until her brother comes. Then, of course, she belongs to him since he is her true sire. You did bring him, didn't you?"

"I'm right here," Julian's voice arrived two seconds before his body did, and I turned with a curse.

"Fuck. I told you to wait!"

"Too late." He spared me a quick glance then returned his glare to Dorian.

"Darling," Dorian took a step toward Julian, and I grabbed his arm. Dorian stopped and looked at my hand with consideration. I didn't release him, and he didn't take another step. "Julian, I knew you'd come."

"Don't, Dorian. We are over."

"You don't mean that."

Hoping their little lover's quarrel would be enough of a distraction, I released Dorian's arm and took a step toward the bedroom and Lily. However, Dorian was too quick and much too smart.

"That's not going to work. I'm disappointed in you for thinking I could be so easily distracted, Preston."

"As usual, you're acting like a spoiled brat, Dorian. You think just because you want something you can have it without concern for anyone else's feelings. My sister won't be your pawn any longer. No matter what you do, whom you harm or kill, I cannot, *will not* return the love you desire. I'd rather die than allow you to keep Lily as your slave any longer . . ." Julian's voice cracked as if he were on the verge of tears.

I glanced at him. *Don't fold on me now, man.*

He swallowed, and his Adam's apple bobbed. "And me." He shook his head. "You locked me up and fed me drugs."

"It was for your own good, darling."

"How was that good for me?" Julian asked, and Dorian looked down at the floor as though he were pondering that question. "You can't make me love you, Dorian. But you know there are a ton of other guys out there who *could* love you. It's a new, modern world. Men like you and me are everywhere. You don't need to hide behind my sister any longer. Just let us go. It's been a fun ride." Julian rubbed his temples at his blunder. "Well, up until the last few decades. But, Dorian, it's over. I can't be your lover any longer. My sister doesn't deserve to live a life pretending to be your wife just so society will think you're the *perfect* family man."

"There are plenty of gay men in the city," I added. "Plenty. Let Lily and us go, and we won't cause you any problems. We can all just move on with our lives."

Just then, a sudden burst of commotion came from outside, and Dorian smiled. "Ah, Malik is finally here." And as if he hadn't heard a word either Julian or I had said, and without warning, he swung his arm out, slamming it into the side of my head. I flew backwards from the force of the blow.

Julian took three steps, closing the gap, his fists ready to pummel. He took a swing, clipping Dorian right in the jaw. Dorian rubbed at it then hit Julian in the chest, sending him across the room.

"It pains me to no end to have to do that to either of you. But you didn't really think I would just stand here and let you beat me to death or take away what's mine, did you? And I truly don't believe that you and your group outside are just going to allow me to walk away from this. The minute I let my guard down, you'll have me beheaded."

I glanced at the empty wall where the sword had been years ago, wishing it still hung there.

"Dorian, you found love after me, didn't you?" I yelled to him as he turned to walk back to where Lily was. I got to my feet and lunged at his back. My arms were around his neck, squeezing in an instant, but he threw me off as if I were no more than a young human boy. Gage appeared in the room and tackled Dorian to the floor. Finally.

"What took you so long?" I asked.

"Goons outside," he croaked as Dorian shoved him off and they both scrambled to their feet. Gage walloped Dorian in the stomach, and Dorian hunched over in pain but regained his stance almost immediately, hurtling his body right back at Gage.

The two wrestled on the ground, and I glanced around to see where Julian was, only to see him heading toward the bedroom. I wanted to go with him. I wanted to be the one to rescue my love, but I had to let him go save her while he had the chance. I opened drawer after drawer, searching for something sharp. I opened the cupboard next to the oven, and there it was, a wooden block full of all sorts of knives. I grabbed the largest one in the block and hurried back to the two wrestling on the floor. They were pretty evenly matched, and I didn't think Gage was going to be able to take Dorian, until I saw his hands grip Dorian's throat and squeeze. Dorian fought, clawing at Gage's arms. I knew Gage would never kill him that way, but it gave me the opportunity to do what needed to be done. I stood over my maker with the knife raised and ready to slice at his throat and sever his head from his body when his eyes found mine and held my gaze. I froze. My mind became overwrought with emotions that had no business being there. Dorian had given me a new life and now I was about to end his.

"Do it!" Gage shouted, still squeezing. "Do it now, dammit! What are you waiting for?"

But I stood, frozen, hurtled back to a time when Dorian had been a gentle soul, eager to please me and attend to my every whim. Though I'd never loved him the way he wanted me to, I couldn't deny the affection I'd had for him and . . . I couldn't bring myself to lower that knife and end his life. Dorian recognized my dilemma and grinned at me, even with Gage's hands around this throat. Then he gazed into my eyes and forced out, "I cannot deny you. I release them to you."

Gage let go of him with one hand to take the blade from me, and in that instant, Dorian disappeared from beneath him.

Gage got to his feet just as the others piled into the room. "Fuck, man! What were you waiting for?"

I shook my head in total disbelief at my lack of courage and the shock of what Dorian said to me. Then I hung my head and let the knife fall to the floor. "I couldn't do it."

Gage nodded. "It's okay. I get it," he said in a soft voice and then picked up the blade I'd dropped.

When I looked up, I watched Julian walk out of the bedroom, carrying Lily in his arms. She was draped in a blanket. She didn't look well. I ran to them, and he handed her over to me. I sank to the floor and cradled her in my arms, so happy to have her back. She was unconscious, and her breathing was labored.

"Where is he?" Lane asked.

"Gone," Gage said, shaking his head. "Just gone."

"I don't sense him anywhere," Julian added, and I closed my eyes, already knowing without using any sensory abilities that Dorian was long gone, far from any of our abilities to sense him. No one gave me any flack for not going through with killing him. I suspected they all knew how difficult it was to kill one's maker. Lane and Cian hadn't killed theirs, though they had managed to secure her and stop her from wreaking any more havoc in their lives.

Dorian was gone. Who knew when or if he would return? Could I be certain that Lily and Julian would be safe from him or was this just another tactic to catch us off guard? Was he truly gone? Would he end all the prostitution drug peddling? One thing I was certain of was that someday, Dorian would return. He was in my blood. The Dorian I'd known had always been a man of his word, especially when it was a promise given to me. Dorian may love Julian, but he'd loved me first, and I wanted to believe that, because of that love, that strong bond we'd share forever, he would always put me before his own happiness.

# CHAPTER 29

Lily

*A* blissful, peaceful, floating-in-nothing darkness enveloped me. The pain I'd experienced from the silver had been unbearable. Never before had I experienced something so powerful and agonizing. But the agony of that pain was gone now, leaving me with this heavenly euphoria. Except there was no white light encouraging me to embrace it or head toward it. That story of people heading toward the light on their way to heaven must have been a myth, unless . . .

*Wait.*

*Was I in hell?*

*I had done nothing to deserve an eternity in hell. I'd never asked to be turned into a vampire. I'd never killed anyone. I did take blood from unsuspecting humans, but not one had ever died because of me. No. This peaceful, serene state soaring through my spirit couldn't be coming from hell. Plus, I was sure hell had to be a lot worse than this. Because this was too peaceful.*

*My spirit lived.*

*I sighed with relief. Even in my vampiric state, I had kept my spirit. I glanced down at myself. I was naked. The gown I'd worn had been ripped from my body by Dorian leaving me with nothing on. Could I enter heaven naked? I placed my hand over my privates and my arm across my breasts to shield them. But maybe this was how everyone entered heaven. After all, we come into this world naked, shouldn't we leave it that way, as well? I wished I could have said goodbye to Preston and Julian before I passed on to the next life.*

*But I didn't feel as though I was in heaven or hell.*

*Just a tranquil nothingness.*

*So this was death? I'd always wondered if it would be as soothing as this. With no concerns, no worries, just a spirit floating through space without a care.*

*Except . . . I had thoughts.*

*My brain still functioned. Surely one's brain would cease all earthly activity once they were dead, or at least transform into something else, join a collective of related souls or become a star in the universe or something. Did a star have thoughts?*

A FOREIGN SOUND invaded my subconscious mind, interrupting my tranquility—and my mental rambling.

I heard voices.

My tongue tasted blood. My eyes slowly opened and then closed. The light was too bright. I blinked. And blinked again. The third time, I kept my lids open to see beautiful dark eyes staring down at me as my taste buds soared with delight when I realized I suckled at Preston's wrist. His blood tasted so good.

"There you are. Not too much." He tried to tug his arm away, but I latched on to it.

*NO!* I panicked.

His blood was my lifeline.

"It's okay. You can let go. I have more for you right here. You need some human blood now, but I didn't want you to wake up to a plastic bag." It took me a minute to process what he was saying, but once my brain accepted the concept, I released my hold on his wrist, and he removed it from my lips, immediately replacing it with an unappealing plastic straw. But I took it, knowing I needed it.

"That's good. Drink. The more blood you ingest, the faster the silver will be obliterated from your system."

When the bag of blood was empty, he took it away. I looked around the room. Everyone stood around, watching. I was on Preston's bed, and I felt very self-conscious with everyone there. But I guess I'd been pretty sick from the silver. My body still shivered from the poison killing all my blood cells. The comforter was pulled up around my neck, but I was still so cold.

"I have another bag right here. I warmed it up in the microwave." A female voice. I looked up to see the petite one, Maggie, smiling at me.

"The more you take, the faster you'll heal." Preston stuck the straw into the plastic film and then placed it at my lips.

My brother came to stand next to me. He placed his hand on top of mine.

*Julian.*

I said his name in my head. There was something I needed to discuss with him. What was it? Something about . . . a dream I'd had. But that was all I could remember as my mind went blank. I pulled the straw from my mouth. "Julian." The sound of my own voice seemed so foreign to me. So low and scratchy.

"Shhh. Drink, get strong, Lil." He grew silent, sorrowful, and the sadness in his eyes was almost too much to bear. I worried that he was upset about Dorian. What had happened to Dorian? Was he dead? Did Preston kill him? Was that why Julian was so sad? How did we get here anyway? Then he added, "I'm so sorry." He hung his head and squeezed my hand.

I frowned and pushed the bag away. "For wha—?"

I couldn't continue because it hurt too much to speak, but I couldn't imagine what he would be sorry for.

"We'll talk when you're well," he said. He looked good. Strong. Healthy. The healthiest I'd seen him in years.

He glanced at Preston. "I should go."

"No," I croaked out like an old frog. I never wanted him to leave me. He was my rock. My one constant in this messed-up world. I needed his strength beside me. He was the reason I had endured Dorian for all those years.

"Okay. But no more talking for you until you can sit up. By the way,"—Julian glanced at Preston and gave me a smile—"this is quite a guy you have here. I approve. Not that you ever needed my approval. After all, you're the big sis."

Everyone that lived with Preston stood around. When one of the women, the one with long, blonde hair, saw I noticed her, she came forward. "We all just wanted to make sure you were okay. We were all so worried."

I must have really been in bad shape. I smiled and mouthed a thank you to her. Vanessa, that was her name.

"You're welcome."

"You're family now. One of us. We're here for you," Maggie said.

"We'll go now and give you some privacy and time to rest and heal," Vanessa added as they headed out of the room.

"Vicious was worried." The female vampire with the short hair winked and lifted the puppy up. I stuck my hand out as the dog licked it. "She wanted to give you a kiss before we go. I'm glad you're okay." She tugged the dog away, and they left the room.

They all seemed to want me here. They were accepting me as one of them. "*One of us*," Maggie had said. I glanced at Preston, who'd sat down next me and stroked his fingers down my arm.

"Hey, I can do better than that bag," the guy who'd been the bouncer at the club said as he came into the room. "If you want it that is. If you do, I got it. It's a hell of a lot fresher than that stuff. Warm, too." He wiggled his eyebrows.

I nodded.

He smiled. "I'm Ari, in case you don't remember." He stuck his arm out toward Preston, and Preston pierced two little holes in his wrist with a quick bite, then Ari held his wrist to my mouth. I was a little timid at first until I got the flow going. "Later, when you're back to normal, I'll take a little of your blood and then we'll be bonded. That way, I'll always be able to find you in case of an emergency. I have a little of everyone in me."

"Yeah," Lane said. "We should nickname you *The Savior*."

"Hmmm . . . I could get used to that. I've saved your ass a few times over the years."

"Okay, let's give her a chance to rest and relax while she drinks Ari's blood." A stranger. Someone I hadn't met before stood beside Preston. He was slightly older-looking than everyone else, maybe in his early thirties when he'd been turned.

"This is Grayson. He's Chelle's dad and our doctor."

A doctor? Chelle's dad? How did that work?

"I think that's enough of Ari's blood. He's beginning to get a little pale." Cian grabbed a chair and placed it directly behind Ari so he could sit.

I stopped sucking at Ari's wrist and ran my tongue over the wounds to heal them. "I'm so sorry, but thank you." I wiped my mouth with my hand, and Preston handed me a towel to finish the job. "I didn't mean to take so much."

"It's okay. I'm used to it. I hope it helped."

"It did. I'm feeling much better."

"Do you mind if I examine you?" Grayson asked.

"No. But I'm sure I'm fine now."

He pulled some sort of machine closer to the bed and put some goopy jelly on a wand that looked similar to a microphone and looked at me. "May I?"

I nodded.

He lifted the cover from my chest just high enough to place the cold, yucky wand between my bosoms so he could move it slowly over the area where my heart and lungs were, all the while looking at the monitor of that machine.

I glanced at the screen. The picture was very fuzzy-looking to me, but then I saw movement.

Beating.

"Is that my heart?"

"Yes. I'm checking to see if there is any more silver close to your heart since this is the place it entered. The further away it travels from this area, the better off you'll be. And I don't see any sign of the silver. That's a good thing. I think we've managed to dilute your veins with enough good, rich blood that you're going to be okay in a few days, maybe sooner." He chuckled. "I keep forgetting how we vampires heal so quickly. I've dealt mostly with humans for so long. Still do." He finished his examination and smiled, adjusting the covers back in place over me. "I'll leave you two alone now." He glanced at Julian. "I mean, you three."

"I'll talk to you later, sis. I'll give you and Preston some time here." Julian got up and left with the doctor.

"I don't know what I would have done if anything had happened to you, Lily. I'm so sorry Dorian did this."

I smiled. "It's not your fault."

"Maybe not, but somehow, I feel responsible."

"Please, don't. Dorian was . . ." I sighed. "Dorian. What happened to him? Did you . . . kill him?"

"No. But he won't hurt you or Julian ever again, I can promise you that. He's gone. I don't know where, but I know he's gone." He lowered his head. "I couldn't bring myself to kill him. I'm sorry, Lily. I'm afraid I'm not the hero you may have thought I was."

I was relieved for some strange reason. The fact that he hadn't killed him was exactly the reason I fell for him in the first place.

"You're braver for not killing him in my opinion. Anyone can kill something they're afraid of, but I think it takes a lot more courage to face your fears and tame them. To overcome something makes you stronger. In here." I pointed to his heart. "You showed humanity by allowing him to live. I respect you for that."

"I find it fucking hard to breathe sometimes just thinking of you," he said, smiling before he kissed me.

"ARE YOU READY?" Preston asked as he came into the bedroom. "Everyone is downstairs, acting like they're starved for human food, but they refuse to start without you."

"Almost," I said as I slipped on the pair of comfy Ugg boots Preston had given me. They were warm and felt like slippers. I'd never owned a pair before, though I'd seen them on many humans. These were black and came up to mid-calf. They went with just about everything, too. They were now my new go-to shoe for everywhere.

"We're having a variety of oyster dishes. Ari found a good deal on them down at Fisherman's Wharf today."

I turned up my nose at the thought of eating an oyster. All I could think of was something resembling a wad of snot.

"Trust me, you'll love them. And if you don't, there's some crab, too."

"Good. I like crab. Not too excited about eating something that looks like a loogie, though."

He laughed.

He held my hand, and we flashed downstairs to the dining room.

"Finally," Lane said, and Vanessa jabbed him in the arm. "Ouch."

She frowned at him. "We have a variety of different dishes. We weren't sure what you liked. Here. There're raw oysters on the half shell with plenty of hot sauce to go with them, oysters Rockefeller, grilled oysters. There's also clam chowder and crab legs."

"But if you don't like seafood, there's also rare prime rib," Lane said. "All vamps love beef. Let's dig in."

The table was impressive with an assortment of different dishes. Especially for vampires, considering that human food wasn't the most important nourishment for them. But it was yummy, and an indulgence that I had a feeling these guys made a special effort to have all the time.

Everybody began passing platters filled with food and scooping things onto their plates. Even my brother. I guess after being held prisoner for so long, this was a real treat for him.

Preston placed two raw oysters on my plate and laughed when I frowned. "Just try it." He put some hot sauce on them and a little horseradish and handed one to me while he picked up the other. "Come on. We'll do it together. On three."

Then everyone started counting.

I smiled, and on three, opened my mouth and let the little bugger slide in. I swallowed and quickly took a swig of the beer from the frosted pint that sat in front of me. "Oh . . . that was just . . . horrible." I laughed, and Preston pressed his lips to mine.

"That a girl." He passed the platter of oysters on and placed a couple of crab legs on my plate, as well as some prime rib. He hand-fed me one of the oyster Rockefellers, and that one wasn't as gross. I sucked on his finger that he left lingering in my mouth until I remembered we weren't alone. I looked around with chagrin but realized no one cared. Preston did silly things to my heart, making me not care about anything except him and how wonderful and sexy he made me feel.

We finished eating, and everybody went his or her separate ways. Preston and I walked into the living area where Cian, Maggie, Gage, and my brother sat relaxing.

Gage got up. "I'm going out."

"Alone?" Cian asked.

"Guess so, since my partner in crime is no longer single. Then he looked at my brother, opened his mouth to speak, and then quickly shut it, shaking his head a little before turning to leave. Before he got out of the room, he stopped and turned back. "Julian."

"Yeah?"

"I suppose we could check out several types of bars if you want to come?"

Julian laughed. "Love to. And, I enjoy both sexes, so whatever type of bar you want is fine by me."

"Oh." Gage let out a sigh of relief. "Good to know."

"Can you give me about twenty minutes, though? I need to talk to Lily first."

"Sure." Gage nodded and headed to the credenza instead and poured himself a drink.

I was glad Julian wanted to talk to me. We hadn't had a chance to really sit and talk about anything since Dorian. Now that he was gone, I didn't miss his presence in my life. I would have thought that I would feel some hole or emptiness if my maker suddenly went far enough away.

Julian motioned to the balcony through the opened double glass doors and walked out there.

"Take your time," Preston said and kissed me on the forehead. "I'll be right here when you're finished."

I joined Julian outside, and he slid the door shut.

"It's beautiful out here," I said.

He nodded.

I looked at him. "Julian. I want you to know, I did everything I could to keep Dorian happy so he wouldn't harm you."

"No. Don't. There are things you don't know," he said. "And I'm sorry, so, so fucking sorry for the past one hundred years of our existence. I never meant for any of that to happen."

"What are you talking about? None of that was your fault. Dorian abducted us. He turned us, made us what we are. It's all his fault."

"That's not entirely true."

"It's not?"

He shook his head. "Things didn't happen quite the way you've always believed. Or were led to believe."

"What are you talking about?"

Julian inhaled deeply. "Dorian didn't attack me."

"What? Of course, he did. I was there, I saw it."

"No, you were compelled to believe that."

I shook my head. "No."

"Please, hear me out. When you and I came home that day, Dorian was in our home. When he approached me, he said he was a friend of our father's. He was just so attractive. I was instantly curious about him. He'd lied, of course, about why he was there. I never questioned his motives. He never needed to use his compulsion on me. I was barely nineteen and very sexually curious. He seduced me. I'm sorry, Lily. I let him do whatever he wanted. I let him kiss me and fondle me. I was young. I'd never had anyone touch me like that before. The fact that he was a man didn't matter. All I knew was he made me feel extremely good. He made me hard. Then, during the heat of the moment, he bit me. At first, it frightened me, but the longer he sucked . . . well, it turned out to be amazing. I wanted more of that experience. He never forced himself on me."

"It's okay. I understand. You were young. You didn't know what he was."

"I asked him to turn me."

"You what?"

"I did. I asked him to turn me. He agreed."

Heat rose up inside of me as I listened to my brother. He had to be making this up.

"Unbeknownst to me, you were under Dorian's compulsion. You had been the entire time and were left to sit and read a book while we were . . . engaged. During my transition, Dorian drained you of too much blood. He planned to let you die. After I completed my turn, I talked Dorian into letting me take care of you since he didn't want you the way he wanted me. So I fed you my blood."

"What?" My gaze snapped to his.

"I made you a vampire. Not Dorian."

"*You* made me? It's your blood that I'm bound to?" The thought came back again. Something I told myself over and over again.

*I only stayed because of Julian.*

I stood with my mouth open like an idiot. I was having a difficult time accepting all of this. Then, something clicked. Things started making more sense. Things like Julian's devotion to Dorian. An admiration I could never quite grasp. I'd always wondered why. I knew one was supposed to fall deeply for their maker. Julian had. I hadn't. I'd thought there was something wrong with me. I'd only stayed because of Julian.

"Dorian knew you'd bond with me, and he used that against you. Threatened you with my demise if you didn't do everything he asked. Being sired by him, I couldn't do anything about it and was forced to compel you into believing that he had sired you so you would listen to him and do whatever he told you to do. But it was actually me telling you what to do."

I could only stare at him; my mouth unable to form any words.

"It was either let you die or let you become his slave. I chose life for you. Please forgive me. I couldn't bear to lose you."

"You could have told me."

"No, I couldn't. If you had known I was your maker and not Dorian, I was afraid you'd try something stupid."

"Like leave?"

He ignored me. "I knew the bond between the two of you wasn't there. But as long as you thought it was and didn't really understand it, that it was *me* you were bound to, you'd believe it and believe that it was just a brother-sister love."

I let silence fill the air between us because I couldn't breathe. I wanted to go inside and take comfort in Preston's arms. My brother had lied to me all these years. I couldn't even look at him. I was so angry. Then, I remembered the dream I'd had back at that house Dorian had taken me to.

"DRINK, LILY." *My brother's voice was so clear in my head, yet so distant. "You'll need to drink if you want to survive. That's it. This is what you need to live." Julian's soothing voice comforted me as his dark, beautiful eyes gazed down at me."*

Only this time, I remembered the part I'd forgotten:

*His smile was wide as he pressed his wrist against my lips, feeding me the much-coveted blood I suddenly craved. Julian's blood.*

JULIAN WAS MY MAKER.

Not Dorian.

And then it hit me. It was all suddenly so clear. Julian had been seduced. Similarly to the way Preston had. If the tables had been turned, if it had been me that Dorian had been attracted to, interested in, and approached the way he had Julian—with the charm, the passion, and the raw, carnal, sensual pleasures—I'm sure I would have had a difficult time resisting, too . . .

And after the transition? I would have done the exact same thing if the tables had been turned. I would have saved my brother the way he saved me.

"I do love you, Lily. You're my sister. Please, say something. I couldn't let you die."

Julian nudged my chin with his finger. "Come on, Lily. Don't hate me. That would be as bad as you dying."

"Yes. I suppose it would be," I said softly, almost a whisper. I did know.

I turned to face Julian and wrapped my arms around his shoulders, tugging as our bodies fell together. "I love you, too. I could never hate you."

"Even knowing what I did?"

"I would have done the same if the situation were reversed."

He sighed. "I'm so relieved." Then he laughed. "You sure it's not the bond?"

"Yes. Well, maybe some of it, but I've always loved you. I believe I would have done the same."

"What's all this love stuff I'm hearing?"

We turned to see Preston standing at the door neither of us had heard open. I stepped back from our embrace and grinned as I returned my gaze to Julian.

"Nothing much. I just have the best little brother in the whole wide world."

# CHAPTER 30

Preston

"So, at least we know you don't care much for oysters."

Lily shook her head. "No. Those are nasty creatures. Like slugs of the water. Except I do like the little pearls they produce."

"I'll have to remember that." I grinned.

"And besides, chocolate makes for such a better aphrodisiac, don't you think?"

Lily's warm, fudge-covered finger slid over my lips, and I opened my mouth to catch it between my teeth in a gentle bite before sucking on it. It was incredible that a woman—correction, *vampire*—such as Lily was here with me. Wanting me. I'd had my share of females, but none that I enjoyed as much as Lily. None of them had ever taken me to the levels of pure bliss that she did.

She'd given me more pleasure in the past hour than I'd ever had in my entire experience with any other woman. She was playful, and I loved how she shuddered when I placed little feather-light kisses over her breasts. And how she climaxed while I sucked and teased her nipples with my tongue. No woman had ever climaxed for me so easily before.

When I'd confessed to Lily that I'd found out that Julian was her maker and hadn't told her, I didn't think she would forgive me for keeping the truth about her and her brother from her, even for the short time I'd known. But she did. She'd forgiven me, saying that she understood. And she loved that I had the patience and courage to wait and let Julian tell her since I'd worried she would be upset about it.

I held my chocolate-laced finger up in front of her mouth, and she opened, taking it, sucking, returning the fun experience. I moaned at the sensation. I was already as hard as steel, but when she wrapped her hand around my hard-on and caressed me gently, teasing me as she rubbed her thumb over the tip where moisture had already accu-mulated as a testament to my excitement, it felt as if I grew another few inches.

We were both naked in the middle of my bed. I placed my finger under her chin as she stroked me and pulled her face up to mine as I gazed into her eyes. Yes, they were the same as mine, but not because of Dorian, and on a lot of levels, I liked that. I'd been okay with it when I thought that Dorian had sired her, but knowing he hadn't was much better.

I needed her. Needed her from the moment she entered my life. I understood it. And no matter how long it seemed to take to finally come to this point in our lives, I knew there was nothing that would ever keep us apart.

I leaned in, seeking her lips, needing her mouth, her tongue to meld with mine, to let the sweet nectar of her taste take me away to somewhere peaceful yet exciting.

I gently pushed her backwards. The bowl of chocolate and rasp-berries fell to the floor with a crash, and she giggled as I spread her legs, my cock instantly missing the sweet stroking attention she'd been giving it. I positioned myself on my knees between her thighs and pulled her legs up, resting her ankles on my shoulders. She was beautiful. Her smile inviting. Her pussy glistened. I teased her entrance with the tip of my erection and inhaled her arousing scent. A few more circles over her clit, and then I plunged into her. She moaned with pleasure, and I groaned at the tightness of her walls surrounding me.

I pulled up, almost completely out so that only the tip of me was in her. I wanted to feel the pleasure of the descent back into her because it was always so amazing. But she became impatient and thrust up toward me.

"Preston," she huffed out with little pants. "More, harder, I need more. I need you."

I needed to please her.

I thrust back inside, taking pleasure in the way her tight walls caressed me again. Then I pulled out again before slamming hard against her. And again. I lost control and let my cock take over as if it had its own agenda.

Lily reached her arms up, latched on to her legs, and tugged herself into me, taking me as far as I could go until my balls pressed against her, the gentle nudging sensation on my testicles sending me into another realm of pleasure. I couldn't hold on any longer, and I burst into her just as something made a loud cracking noise, and we fell a few feet, yet we were still on the bed.

"What the fuck?"

"Oh, no! What happened?" she asked.

"It appears, my sweetness,"—I kissed her nose—"that we broke the bed."

I OPENED my eyes and smiled at the sight of Lily sound asleep beside me. My cock hardened just looking at her. I smiled as I remembered how the force of our lovemaking had broken the bed. The mattress was still half on the floor and half on the frame. Tonight, we'd have to purchase a new one. We'd pick it out together. I was looking forward to that.

But I had to piss. I stepped up from the mattress as my foot sank into something squishy, and glanced down to see my fudge-covered toes. "Yuck," I whispered, not wanting to wake Lily. I hopped to the bathroom on one foot and washed off the chocolate then took the much-needed leak. I headed back to bed, but I didn't want Lily to wake up and step in the sticky mess we'd had so much fun with earlier, so I yanked on a pair of shorts and a T-shirt. Then I grabbed the bowl and headed downstairs to find something to clean up the rug.

As I entered the kitchen, I heard someone rummaging through the fridge. Yes, Ari was up, just the man I needed.

"Ari, what do we have that will take chocolate fudge out of carpet fiber?"

The head that popped up from the refrigerator grinned at me, but it wasn't Ari's.

"Dorian."

If he thought I'd show fear or even shock that he was here, he was wrong.

"What the fuck are you doing here?" I said, keeping my voice calm. How did he even get in? Then I remembered . . . The privileges of sires went beyond what was normal, and they apparently didn't need an invitation to enter the homes of their offspring. And this mansion housed two of Dorian's now, making the task even easier.

"Preston. Good. I'm glad it was you who found me. Anyone else would have had my ass thrown out of here faster than you could say, rumplestanskin."

"Rumpelstiltskin," I corrected.

"Right. I was never any good with those silly nursery rhythms. I suppose the world is better off that I wasn't able to father any human children."

"It's a fairytale."

He waved that away.

"What do you want?"

He took a deep breath before exhaling slowly. I didn't find him as threatening as I thought I would. Something in my gut told me that he wasn't there to hurt anyone. Or steal anybody away. So I let him speak.

"I just wanted to see you one more time. I can't tell you how much gazing upon you soothes me. Gives me memories I'd forgotten all about. I wanted a chance to explain myself. Things were difficult for me when I left you. I knew I had to. I loved you enough to let you go."

"You said that in your letter."

"Yes, but I don't think you really understood how painful it was to leave."

"Why should I care, Dorian? You left. I haven't seen you for over two hundred years until last week. Why should I care now about your feelings when you never considered mine?"

He closed his eyes and pressed his lips tightly together. When he opened them, he looked at me.

"I did consider yours." His eyes glistened with wetness, and his voice cracked with a sob, but he took another deep breath and steadied himself. I placed the chocolatey bowl in the sink and grabbed a bag of blood from the fridge. I handed it to him and reached for another for myself. *Blood and tears*, I mused. The sweat would have to come later when I was with Lily. I pulled out a chair for Dorian and gestured for him to sit. When he did, I sat in another.

"That was why I left in the first place," he continued. "As much as it pained me to admit it, I had to come to terms with the plain and simple fact that you were not a gay man, no matter how much I wanted you to be. I knew you needed something I could never give you. If I had stayed, I would have never been able to cope with your lust for females. I could never just sit back and watch that. I left for you. I gave you up because it was the best thing for you. It killed me, knowing that you weren't as invested in us as I was and that your thoughts would always be on another."

Now it was my turn to take a deep breath because I couldn't become that same weak man I was back then and give in to his charms. The control he had over me was uncanny. I couldn't allow myself to feel sorry for him, even though I did. The wall I'd built up was cracking, and I needed to find the courage deep within me to stand up to him. So I dug deep down to find the hardness I needed. For Lily's sake. For Julian's sake, too.

189

"That's really touching, Dorian. Except why the fuck did you keep Julian and Lily against their will for so long?"

He smiled. "When I left you, I roamed around mindlessly for years. I'd go for weeks without ingesting any blood. I didn't care what happened to me. I didn't realize it would hurt so much. The loneliness." The sorrow behind his eyes was killing me. "And I was in mourning, I guess. When I first set eyes on Julian, something ignited inside of me again. A desire that I hadn't felt since I left you. He is so much like you, you know." He smiled. "I was instantly captivated by his beautiful features. He was irresistibly gorgeous. But he . . . well, let's just say I didn't want to lose him. When he had that stupid affair, there was only one thing I could do. I couldn't go through that pain again."

He straightened in his seat and caught my eyes with his. "But I came here to tell you that I've come to terms with everything. If nothing else, I am a man of my word, and I gave Julian his freedom. His sister was never really mine so, of course, she is free, as well. I managed to find another after you. Perhaps, it will happen again someday."

I drained the blood from the bag and threw it in the trash as the door to the kitchen opened. Dorian and I looked up to see Gage. His eyes went wide, and his body tensed, ready to pounce on Dorian. I held up my hand in a gesture to relax, and he stood still, but his eyes narrowed with concern.

"Everything okay in here?" he asked.

"Yeah. Dorian was just leaving," I said and stood. When Dorian got up, he said, "One more thing before I leave."

"What's that?"

"I've sold the tower. They'll start renovations on it within the week. All my belongings are gone from it. I've also resigned from all my positions with the city and ended all the drug and trafficking operations of Sweet's Delicacies. I'm leaving San Francisco."

"Where will you go?" I wasn't sure I wanted to know, but for Lily's sake, I thought I'd better ask.

He shrugged. "Europe, I think. I'll disappear for a few decades or so, start a new life there. I've done it before. Before your time." He chuckled. "Take care of yourself, Preston."

"And you," I said as he vanished from sight.

"Fuck, man. I thought we were going to have another go at him."

I sucked in my lips. "I think we've seen the last of Dorian for a while."

"You sure?"

"I'm sure." I knew in my gut. For some reason, I trusted Dorian. "He'll keep his word." I was certain of it.

I ran into Julian in the hallway on my way back upstairs to Lily. Cian had offered him a permanent room in the mansion, and that was okay with me. It gave Lily an opportunity to stay close to her brother because I wasn't letting her out of my sight, ever.

"Hey, I uh . . . Dorian was just here," I said.

"I know. I saw him."

"You did?"

"He came to say goodbye. I knew he would. I knew he'd never be able to just vanish. But . . . he won't be back. He gave me his word."

I nodded and patted Julian on the back as we walked back to our respective rooms. Julian and I were brothers of a sort. *In more than one way*, I mused.

# EPILOGUE

Preston

*I* pulled down the comforter and quietly slipped in beside Lily. Propping up on my elbow, I rested my head on my hand and watched her sleep. How did I get so lucky? I'd come from nothing. Crippled and broke. And then a shitstorm had hit, taking me on a wild ride, and transforming me into something better. I never regretted my life as a vampire. I embraced it full force. Was thankful for it even. Every facet of it had been a miracle. Dorian had seen to that. He'd recognized something in me that I never saw as a human. He may have been a monster for a period, but he'd never been anything but my savior. There was good in him. I saw it. I knew Julian saw it. That's why I couldn't kill him.

"We'll have a good life together, Lily. I promise. And I'll always love you," I whispered softly, and she stirred a little but didn't wake. "I love you, Lily. I never told you. You knew weeks ago. I guess I knew it, too, but I never said it." It was true, I loved her so fucking much it hurt to think about what might have happened to her. And it felt amazing to tell her how much I loved her. But since she was sound asleep, she couldn't hear me.

I wanted her to wake up so I could tell her but I knew she needed her rest. I just couldn't keep my hands off her. I traced my finger over her shoulder, down her arm, circled her elbow before moving down to her wrist, and to her delicate and dainty fingers. Before I knew it, I was skimming my hand over the soft flesh of her abdomen. Within a few minutes, she slowly opened her beautiful eyes.

"Hey." She smiled. "What are you doing?"

"Watching you sleep."

"It felt more like you were trying to rouse me. Or maybe *arouse* me." She chuckled and ran her fingers slowly down my chest to my stomach, mimicking my actions, but she stopped right at the tip of my already rock-hard cock.

"I like the way you think." I glanced at the one-way glass in the window facing the city. The sun was just coming up, and the rest of the household would be heading to bed. I hoped. "Come with me." I grabbed her hand and tugged her up.

"But I'm naked."

"That's okay. So am I." I grinned. "No one will see us. I promise." I loved how modest she was. Most of the vampire females I'd been with could have cared less who saw them naked and pranced around, proudly showing themselves off. But not my Lily.

I stuck my arm under her legs and lifted her, cradling her in my arms as we dematerialized.

"Where are we?" she asked when I placed her back on her feet.

"This room is called the sunroom." I locked the door and flicked on a red light. The red light was Lane's idea, and a good one if you asked me. It was the indicator that the room was occupied and that the occupants did not want to be disturbed.

She looked at the light. "I suppose that means privacy?"

"See? I knew you were smart." I grinned.

She chuckled and slowly looked around, absorbing every inch of the garden—the multiple bushes of roses in various colors, the daisies. The new tulips.

193

She took her time and looked around, finally looking up, she gasped and hid behind me.

I laughed. "It's just an illusion. A hologram that makes the ceiling look and move as though it's the sky outside, but it can't hurt you."

"Wow. This is amazing."

I took her hand. "Come with me." I led her to the jetted tub as she continued to look up all the way. I stopped in front of the spa that was fairly new and pushed a button on the wall, turning on the jets as bubbles and foam floated to the surface.

"Ever had sex in a hot tub?"

"You know I haven't." If vampires could blush, her cheeks would have probably turned a gorgeous shade of crimson.

"Right." I grinned and stepped into the warm, steamy pool and reached out my hand. "Come on, Lily. It feels good." She took my hand and stepped in.

My arms immediately went around her, and I tugged her onto my lap as she draped her arms gently around my neck.

"You know, I love the fact that I am the only man you've ever been with. I should thank Dorian for that."

"Is that because I don't have anyone to compare you to?" she teased. "I mean, for all I know, you could be a terrible lover and I wouldn't have any idea, would I? And this,"—she wrapped her fingers around my hard erection and I trembled from within—"could be really small compared to other men."

"I assure you, it's not!" I huffed out with a huskiness to my voice, and she laughed at my sudden need to defend the size of my manhood. I coughed, choking on my laugh.

"But how would I ever know?" she smirked.

I narrowed my eyes. "Woman, you need to stop before I find a reason to dunk you under before proving myself to you."

Her eyes widened. "You wouldn't dare."

"I wouldn't?" I shoved her backwards until she was fully submerged under the water. I didn't hold her there long, just enough to get her hair and face wet. When I pulled her back up, my eyes grew lustful as my cock grew in size at the beautiful sight of a wet and drip-ping Lily. I wanted to be inside of her so badly.

She came up laughing. Her smile infectious. "You are going to be sorry, mister." She splashed water at my face as she giggled. I had no choice but to reach out and grab her around the waist. Lifting her, I set her on the edge of the tub. Her beautiful brown eyes, laced with the golden glow of arousal, gazed into mine.

Spreading her legs, I dipped down and swiped my tongue up the length of her core. She shuddered now as her fingers tangled in my hair, urging me on, I had no problem with that as my tongue dipped, licked, and pressed against her clit. As I slipped two fingers inside her tight canal, I closed my eyes and groaned with pleasure at the wetness I found there. I couldn't stand it any longer and slipped my tongue down to penetrate and taste her sweet nectar reserved just for me and said a silent thank you to Dorian. I held on to her thighs as she shook with pleasure. When I was sure she'd come a couple of times, I kissed my way back up to her neck, then gazed at her lovely face. She was so beautiful, and I was so lucky.

"I love you, too," she said in a low voice as she stared back into my eyes.

"You heard me tell you when you were sleeping?"

She nodded. "I did."

I swiped back some wet strands of hair from her face. "I love you. I love you. I love you. I love you."

She giggled and pressed her lips to mine.

"You're safe now, Lily. Always safe with me."

Her legs trembled as I held her ass cheeks and tugged her back into the warm water. I kissed her neck, her chin, her cheek, and then her lips. She returned every single emotion I gave. I stopped and gazed at her, wanting to see her face, her eyes, the glow I'd thought she'd gotten from Dorian only to find was from her brother. A glow so much like mine.

Our eyes, our commonality, Lily, Julian, and me. We'd all been possessed by Dorian at one time or another.

I sat on the edge of the pool and tugged Lily onto my lap as she sank down on top of me. Once again, I became lost in the sensation of her tight walls as we both reached that peak of ecstasy together again.

She breathlessly leaned against me, and we sat there for a short while until I remembered something she'd told me. There was something I needed to show her.

"Come on. Let's get out of here."

"Okay. Why the sudden rush?" Her eyes widened in alarm as if she thought I'd heard someone coming in.

"No rush. I just want to show you something."

"We don't have any clothes."

I grabbed her hand, tugged her across the room to a door, and opened it. I reached inside the closet and grabbed a couple of towels and handed one to her. "Here. You can dry off."

"Thanks. She took the towel and held it against her face. "Mmmm . . . it smells like a garden of roses." She smiled and rubbed the towel over her wet body. "Can we go back to the room first? I don't want to parade around the house in a towel."

"No need. Here." I handed her a fluffy, white robe.

She laughed and shrugged into the robe. "You knew these were here all along?"

I nodded. "Let's go."

I grabbed her around the waist and held her close to me as we disappeared and then materialized a few seconds later. I let go of her. Her brown eyes grew wide—the widest I'd ever seen them. The smile on her face was priceless.

"Preston. This is amazing. Wow." She twirled around, looking everywhere, and ran her hand over the comfortable pale blue loveseat and then hurried over to the two plush, gold recliner chairs by the fireplace all while she took in the walls of the room. "There are so many books." She looked up at the three-story-high wall of shelves packed with books that graced three of the walls in the room.

"Cian and Lane have been collecting books for a long time. Some of these are first editions. But I'm sure there are plenty of books that are more recent. Maybe even some romance novels."

"Wow. And look how high the shelves go. Have I died and gone to heaven?"

"I hope not. Not yet, anyway. I need you with me for at least another thousand years."

"Only a thousand?"

I shrugged. "Give or take a few."

"Preston, I could live in this room and be content for the rest of my life without ever having to leave." She laughed. "And look. There's a ladder that slides along the shelves. I wouldn't even need to ask for help to get one of those books that are way up there." She pointed to the top shelf that was about twenty feet above us.

"Do you think you could find something in here you might like to read? Perhaps one of those erotica novels you mentioned? Maybe you could read it to me?" I waggled my eyebrows at her.

"That might be kind of fun."

"If I'd known that it would only take a few books to make you happy, I'd have shown you this room a long time ago."

"*You* make me happy." She came toward me and wrapped her arms around my waist as I tucked her in close to me. "The books? They're a nice bonus."

I grinned and squeezed her a little tighter. I was happy, truly happy for the first time in my very long life, and it was all because of Lily.

KEEP READING **for a sneak peek at Protected by a Vampire.**

# SNEAK PEEK AT PROTECTED BY A VAMPIRE, BOOK 5 IN THE IMMORTAL HEARTS OF SAN FRANCISCO SERIES

## Chapter 1

### Gage

**Five Years Ago**

*A* rumble developed deep in the pit of my gut, stabbing at the walls of my stomach like I'd swallowed a jagged stone. That coupled with the proliferated dizziness swirling in my head from low blood sugar caused me to stop and take a few deep breaths. Hunger pains were a bitch.

A shrill whistle to my left caught my attention.

"Hey sugar, you want some action tonight?"

I eyed the elder, weather-beaten face of the woman standing by the doorway leading to some offbeat nightclub that most likely hadn't been graced by a sober person in months.

I blinked at her. My vision was slightly blurred from the vertigo caused by the lack of sustenance, but was she really wearing a purple see-through top that did a piss poor job of hiding her sagging tits and fishnet tights that had more holes in them than a cheese grater, under a skirt that barely covered her lady parts and was way too short for her Twiggy sized legs? I blinked again. Yep, she was.

Slick, black hair hung in tight ringlets to her shoulders, making her look like she'd slathered a jar of Crisco over her head. Thick, ruby lips smiled at me and hope sparkled in her eyes.

I was hungry, but not that hungry. I was no great catch, but this one was definitely out of my league, like about forty feet below it.

"No thanks." Not in this lifetime. "Or afterlife, even," I mumbled quietly to myself as I shook my head. No need to hurt the old woman's feelings. It seemed to me that she should have hung up her fishnets and stilettos years ago. But who was I to judge?

"Suit yourself, doll, but I'd love to rub myself ..." she grabbed her tits in her hands and pressed them together and up, showing me what her cleavage probably looked like twenty years ago. Hell, maybe thirty. "... all over those gorgeous blond strands of yours. Plus, you look like you could use some tender loving care, honey."

I shook my head and kept walking, running my hand nervously through my shoulder length, sandy locks. She'd been right about one thing, though. And maybe that was my problem. Maybe it wasn't hunger pains that gnawed at my gut. Maybe it was the lack of—as the elderly woman said—*tender loving care*.

Could she be right?

Don't get me wrong; I never had problems getting laid. But it seemed like every female I came across lately was pretty much an airhead. They were either strung out on drugs or too into themselves and the clothes they wore, or in this last case, weren't wearing. Most had nothing to offer other than their bodies and their blood. No great conversation to spark my interest.

I guess that came with the territory since it was prostitutes and female vamps that usually helped me get my rocks off and provided the nutrition I needed to sustain this miserable life I led. I hadn't been interested in anything lasting and meaningful. Wasn't even sure I deserved anything permanent anyway. But I sure as hell wasn't going anywhere near the old has been I'd just walked passed.

If I wasn't looking for any kind of lasting relationship, why did I feel so empty? I liked my freedom, but there was something keeping me from enjoying it, something I couldn't quite place.

When I reached the corner of the block, I headed south toward the beach. Surely there would be someone who would spark my interest along the way. An eerie silence swirled around me like someone stole the noise out of the night air on this deserted street. Not many people out this time of the night. I continued my trek, and now hunt, for another meal, but as before, the street was deserted, not even a horn blaring in the far off distance. San Francisco was a large city; normally you could hear horns blowing and engines roaring all the time.

But not this night.

A weird feeling crept over me as I headed down a dark and vacant street near North Beach. The ache in my chest worsened. I swiped the back of my hand over the sweat beading at my brow. I frowned as my toe crashed into a rusted and empty soup can, sending it several feet into the gutter. I stopped and glanced over at two trash cans toppled over by the curb; broken beer bottles, dirty diapers, moldy Styrofoam containers all spilled out over the sidewalk. I wasn't a humanitarian or anything—I wasn't even human—but that just pissed me off. A growl burst from my chest as I picked up the garbage and stuffed most of the swill back inside the cans. I left anything that oozed gooey remnants of someone's dinner or worse ...

A shrill screech grabbed my attention. What the hell was that?

It took a few seconds for the sound to register in my brain, but that had definitely been a scream. The loud crash and another faint scream had me curious about all the ruckus. I rounded the corner, entering a dark alley behind a small neighborhood grocery store. It stunk like cat piss and stale cigarette butts. Not the best spot to be in the wee hours of the night.

A large man had a woman pinned against the brick wall on the other side of a rusted and beat up old baby carriage, a dilapidated suitcase and a pile of old and yellowed newspapers. I sniffed the stale air and it didn't take long for me to recognize his vampirism. Vampires could always detect one another since our blood never smelled the way a human's did. His hand covered the woman's mouth, muting her screams, and his fangs were about to sink into her jugular.

Ordinarily, I didn't get involved in another vampire's business or dinner. We all had to eat. But something about the way he was rough handling her, the way she'd cried out, and the look of hope in her frightened eyes when she saw me round the corner made me want to stop him from drinking her blood.

We didn't need to be brutes. A little compulsion went a long way in making a prospective blood donor feel relaxed and compliant. This young woman didn't seem too eager to give this vampire her blood. And it certainly didn't appear that this guy used any compulsion on her. My guess was he was going to either let her suffer through the fear and then wipe her memory, or he would simply kill her when he finished. That seemed a little barbaric. When I or my brothers took nourishment that was all it was. Satisfying one's bloodlust didn't need to be violent.

This was an act of violence.

And it wasn't acceptable. But there was another element that drove me forward, tugging at my chest ...

The preternatural desire to protect *this* woman.

"Hey! How about you leave her alone!" Not the most persuasive statement I'd ever made, but it got his attention.

He glanced at me, his red flamed eyes ablaze with petulance. One of his hands clutched her long brown hair, pinning her head back as he held her against the wall with his other. "Who do you think you are?"

Like a flash of lightning, I drew closer to them and took an attack stance about a foot away. "Your worst nightmare," I said, baring my own fangs. The female screamed.

"Fuck you! Go get your own meal."

The woman's eyes grew wide with fear and I heard her quick intake of a gasp as her gaze settled on me, a plea for her life evident in her tear-filled orbs. I had about six inches and forty pounds on the guy, but vampires weren't known to possess a lot of fear toward one another and we were all unusually strong. Stronger than any human, that is.

"Not going to happen. This one belongs to me," I lied. I didn't know who the hell she was, but something inside of me didn't want him to have her.

"Who the hell cares?" He tilted his head and grinned, showing off a two-inch, red and black jeweled dagger tattoo on his neck below his right ear. He was dressed in all black; that mixed with those flaming eyes made him look quite ominous. "This isn't a reservations required program, pal."

"Leave her alone."

"Who died and made you boss?" The vampire grinned at me, chuckling at his own stupid joke.

I stood tall, trying to intimidate him with my size. "Don't make me hurt you."

He glanced around the alley, shifted his head to peer behind me, then his deadly gaze landed back on me, still grinning. "You and what army?"

Now I grinned and took an offensive stance. "Let's see what you've got."

He released the woman, shoving her to the ground, and faced me. She was on her hands and knees and quickly pushed her feet behind her, taking a racer's stance.

"Run!" I hissed through gritted teeth, though the order was completely unnecessary as she'd already taken off down the dark alley. I grabbed the vampire by the shoulder, tossing him against the opposite wall.

He quickly got up and growled, showing his fangs, his legs apart, his feet flat on the ground. His fists were up and ready to pound into my face. Then he charged, smacking my back against the wall. He was stronger than I'd anticipated.

I hadn't killed another vampire or human in about three hundred years. In fact, I hadn't even fought another vampire in a few months, but I was fairly confident that I could take him, or at least cause some major damage. I slugged him in the jaw and shoved him backwards. He stumbled, but quickly righted himself. Shaking off my punch, he tore at me again.

I grabbed him around the neck, choking the air out of him when something sharp pierced into my gut and twisted. I released my grip and he stepped back. The blade he held in his hand dripped with blood. My blood. My hands went to my stomach, crimson liquid oozing over my fingers as I sank to the ground.

The vampire bent down and snarled in my face. "You should know better than to interrupt a vampire during a meal, dip shit. Some of us don't rely on our fangs alone. You're lucky I'm in a pretty good mood, otherwise, you may have lost your head tonight. Besides, she was tainted anyway." Then he vanished.

Luckily, my vampirism helped me heal quickly. Except the level of pain I was in was far greater than anything I'd ever experienced before, and I'd been stabbed plenty of times over the years. My gut roiled, like something evil swirled around inside me, grabbing on to each and every cell inside my stomach. The blade must have been coated with poison, some sort of toxic substance strong enough to inflict injury to a vampire. Whatever it was, it was spreading faster than my own blood could coagulate.

I blinked back the sting of tears in my eyes. "Fuck." The cut was deep and blood seeped between my fingers, and dripped down my side to the pavement, prohibiting my ability to teleport out of there and back to the mansion where I lived with my band mates, my brothers.

I glanced down at the wound and wondered if I would heal at all.

Since I had no idea what kind of poison coated that blade, I had no idea if I would even live through the night.

A hand at my shoulder surprised me and I looked up into the face of the woman I'd protected.

"I told you to run." Even *I* could hear the anguish through my words.

She frowned. "I know, but you're bleeding."

I glanced at my abdomen. Blood coated my fingers; my ripped shirt was drenched with red. "Why are you still here? He could have grabbed you again."

"I was afraid he'd kill you. And it looks like he almost succeeded. I couldn't leave you here to die. Besides, I had a great hiding place."

She took off the sheer wrap she was wearing and placed it over my stomach and pressed her delicate, small hands firmly against it, trying to stop the bleeding. Her long golden brown hair flowed down past her shoulders and over her breasts, partially covering her face. She flicked one side back over her shoulder and bit her bottom lip while she stared at my stomach. Then her gaze found mine. She had the most stunning green eyes I'd ever seen and I swear I was drowning in their emerald tranquility. I could have stayed caught in her gaze, content to live out the rest of my life there. Euphoria took me and I drifted, floating in a sea of serenity.

"There's so much blood. You need medical attention."

The sound of her voice, filled with concern, brought me to my senses. "I'll be okay. You need to get out of here. He might come back," I managed to choke out through the pain.

She glanced behind her then back at my abdomen and the blood. "I can't leave you. I'll never be able to live with myself if I walk away and you died. Let me take you somewhere."

I shook my head. "No. No hospital. I told you, I'll be okay." The last thing I needed was human doctors witnessing my quick recovery. The only doctor I trusted was Grayson, since he was a vampire too, and would take care of my wound discreetly. Problem was, he worked at City General Hospital, and there were at least two others between here and there. No way would I be able to convince this young woman to trek me all the way across town without a damn good reason. And the fact that I'm a vampire won't cut it, since, well, I can't tell her that.

I tried to sit up so I could assess the damage for myself. "You don't need to stay here. Go before he comes back."

"You don't look okay. And if he comes back to find you still here bleeding out, he might finish what he started. Can you walk if you hold on to me?"

She had a point. I didn't like the idea of staying there in the alley hemorrhaging. It might be a while before I healed enough to get out of there on my own. The last thing I needed was for that vampire to come back or worse, another human stumbling upon me and wanting to be a Good Samaritan, calling 911. My chances were most likely better with this woman. Though, as I gave her another glance, she seemed more like a girl, barely old enough to be called a woman. But she was apparently old enough to be out in the middle of the night, alone.

"Maybe. Give me your hand."

She stood, latching onto my arm, helping me up. I leaned my shoulder against the wall, shimmying up to help with my weight. Once I was standing or at least upright but on shaky legs, she positioned her shoulder under my arm and we headed out of the alley. She had a good height about her; enough that I didn't need to crouch down to lean on her ... and she smelled delicious. Not the scent of her blood, though that was enticing enough, but her entire being smelled like mangos and peaches and the palms of her hands felt as smooth as cream against my wrist as she held on to me. I didn't pay too much attention to where we headed after we left the alley.

I wasn't positive, but since she wasn't afraid of me, I didn't think she realized I was a vampire. How should I handle the situation? She'd have to invite me inside in order for me to enter any building she would be taking me to. If I told her this, she might get scared.

A short while later, we stood in front of a heavy black door. As she placed her hand on the knob, she turned to me.

"Come in here and be quiet. I have a nosy, old busy-body of a neighbor. I don't want to wake her up and have her come out here asking questions." She led me through the heavy door and down a corridor. We stopped in front of another door and she opened it.

"In here," she whispered. "Go lie on that sofa." She pointed at a plush green sofa against the wall, beneath a row of windows. Her words were enough of an invite to allow me through the apartment entrance. She grabbed a blanket from the back of a chair and placed it on the couch, then my vision blurred to the point where I couldn't see. All I remembered from that moment was sinking down onto something soft and then I was out.

**Continue Reading Protected by a Vampire**

# ALSO BY SUSAN GRISCOM

*Paranormal Romance*

*Vampires*

**Immortal Hearts of San Francisco Series**

*Tempted by a Vampire*

*Captivated by a Vampire*

*Rocked by a Vampire*

*Possessed by a Vampire*

*Protected by a Vampire*

*Bewitched by a Vampire*

*Urban Fantasy*

**The Sectorium Series**

*Ignite the Flame*

*Reflect the Flame*

*Tame the Flame*

**A Gypsy's Kiss**

**Wet Kisses**

*Contemporary*

**Sand and Sunset Series**

*Broken Wide Open*

**The Beaumont Brothers Series**

*Beautifully Wounded*

*Beautifully Used*

*Beautifully Undone*

*Shared Worlds*

**Michelle Fox's Blood Courtesans**

*Refrain – Neriza – A Blood Courtesans Vampire Paranormal Romance*

**Dark Moon Falls**

**Dark Moon Falls: Cooper**

**Dark Moon Falls: MILO**

*TUCKER – Currently in the Dark Moon Falls III Anthology. It will release on its own January 2022*

# EMOTIONAL STUFF

Possessed by a Vampire contains a lot of stuff that I'm sure a lot of my readers are not used to reading in my books. I have to say that this was a difficult book for me to write. Not because of the subject matter, but because it was extremely complicated. I had to do a lot of research throughout (which I usually do anyway, but more so in this book) because of the drug and human/vampire trafficking. I hope I got everything right.

I must give a huge thank you to my two editors. Michelle Olson and Tami Lund. You ladies were quick to pick up on anything amiss and really helped make this book shine. I think the world of both of you and want to send out huge hugs to you. I love you both to the moon.

Thank you to my dear friend and proof reader, Trallee Mendonca. You really know your stuff and I am so very grateful to call you my friend.

My beta readers, Author Tami Lund, Anna Dase, and Ellie McLove were awesome and extremely helpful and hopefully I got all your suggestions down and everything works.

A huge thank you to my street team, you all build me up and

always make me feel so special. Thank you for all that you do. You are always in my heart.

I can't write a book without thanking my husband for his love and support that he gives me. He cooks dinner when I'm so deep into a story that I can't tear myself away and he does his own laundry—that, in itself is huge.

Thank you, Mom, for your everlasting love.

To my kids and grandkids, I love you!

Lastly, to you, the reader. Much love and thank you for all of your reviews and the support you've shown throughout the years of my writing career. I love you to the moon!!!

Please keep the reviews coming because I love reading your thoughts about my books. Feel free to join my Facebook Fan Page and my Newsletter where you will be the first to see cover reveals, exclusive excerpts, and enter into exclusive contests. Please feel free to shoot me an email at susan@susangriscom.com if you want to talk about my books.

Thank you, again, for reading.

Love and hugs,

Susan

# ABOUT THE AUTHOR

Susan Griscom writes paranormal and contemporary romance. She's hooked on gritty romances and is a huge fan of superheroes and bad boys confronted with extraordinary forces of nature, powers, and abilities beyond the norm mixed with steamy romance, of course.

When she's not writing, she loves spending time with friends, sipping wine or champagne and dancing.

She lives in Northern California with her romantic husband and together they have five great superhero kids and nine mini-superhero grand kids, so far.

Sign up for Susan Griscom's newsletter: http://www.susangriscom.com/newsletter.html
Other ways to follow and learn more.
Susan's Website: http://susangriscom.com

Printed in Great Britain
by Amazon

71559469R00130